PRAISE FOR JOSE[

"Flynn is an excellent

"Flynn propels his plot with potent but ....
— *Publishers Weekly*

Digger
"A mystery cloaked as cleverly as (and perhaps better than)
any John Grisham work." — *Denver Post*

"Surefooted, suspenseful and in its breathless final moments
unexpectedly heartbreaking." — *Booklist*

The Next President
"*The Next President* bears favorable comparison to such
classics as *The Best Man, Advise and Consent* and
The Manchurian Candidate."
— *Booklist*

"A thriller fast enough to read in one sitting."
— *Rocky Mountain News*

The President's Henchman (A Jim McGill Novel)
"Marvelously entertaining." — *ForeWord Magazine*

Tall Man in Ray-Bans

A John Tall Wolf Novel

Joseph Flynn

Stray Dog Press, Inc.
Springfield, IL
2014

Books by Joseph Flynn

The Jim McGill Series
The President's Henchman, *A Jim McGill Novel*
The Hangman's Companion, *A Jim McGill Novel*
The K Street Killer, *A Jim McGill Novel*
Part 1: The Last Ballot Cast, *A Jim McGill Novel*
Part 2: The Last Ballot Cast, *A Jim McGill Novel*
The Devil on the Doorstep, *A Jim McGill Novel*
The Good Guy with a Gun, *A Jim McGill Novel*

McGill's Short Cases 1-3

The Ron Ketchum Mystery Series
Nailed, *A Ron Ketchum Mystery*
Defiled, *A Ron Ketchum Mystery Featuring John Tall Wolf*

The John Tall Wolf Series
Tall Man in Ray-Bans, *A John Tall Wolf Novel*
War Party, *A John Tall Wolf Novel*
Super Chief, *A John Tall Wolf Novel*

The Concrete Inquisition
Digger
The Next President
Hot Type
Farewell Performance
Gasoline, Texas
Round Robin, A Love Story of Epic Proportions
Blood Street Punx
One False Step
Still Coming
Still Coming Expanded Edition
Hangman — *A Western Novella*

Pointy Teeth, Twelve Bite-Size Stories
Insanity°Diary:
A Sixty-Something Couple Takes Shaun T's 60 Day Challenge

Dedication

This book is dedicated to five of my favorite art directors: Dorie, Jim, Ratso, Virginia and Z.

Acknowledgements

Thanks to my first, and second, readers: Catherine, Anne Sue and Cat.

Author's Notes

This is a work of fiction. Neither the characters nor the Native American reservations named in the story are real. The Bureau of Indian Affairs, of course, exists within the United States Department of the Interior, and within the BIA its Office of Justice Services is "responsible for the overall management of the Bureau's law enforcement program," but my research turned up no one who has the job description I gave to John Tall Wolf. This mixture of fact and fiction falls under the heading of literary license. If you're a purist who demands complete realism, I recommend you stick to nonfiction, and good luck finding an author in that field who doesn't make mistakes or omissions.

As to a white male writing about Native American characters, that involves a bit of license, too. From my point of view, that license is rooted in our common humanity. If writers were to focus only on characters who shared their own backgrounds, we would establish a regime of literary apartheid.

AL
**Reader
Discretion
Advised**
Contains Adult
Language

Stray Dog Press, Inc.

Tall Man in Ray-Bans
A John Tall Wolf Novel
Published by Stray Dog Press, Inc.
Springfield, IL 62704, U.S.A.

© Stray Dog Press, Inc., 2012
Author website: *www.josephflynn.com*

Flynn, Joseph
Tall Man in Ray-Bans / Joseph Flynn
207 pg.
ISBN 978-0-9887868-9-9

Publisher's Note
This is a work of fiction. Names, characters, places, and incidents are either the product of the author's imagination or are used fictitiously; any resemblance to actual persons, living or dead, events, or locales is entirely coincidental.

Book design by Aha! Designs

Tall Man
in
Ray-Bans

A John Tall Wolf Novel

CHAPTER 1

Santa Fe, New Mexico — June 26, 1975

Haden Wolf heard an animal growl. Serafina Wolf y Padilla heard a baby squall.

Without exchanging a word, they raced off along the path through the underbrush in the foothills of the Sangre de Cristo Mountains. They ran in the direction of the commotion. Serafina, short and lithe, built for both speed and endurance, was in the lead. Haden, tall and muscular, pounded along behind his wife, watching for hazards on the trail that Serafina avoided instinctively. He also made sure the Winchester he carried didn't discharge accidentally.

The Wolfs had gone out at dawn to gather Rocky Mountain Brookmint. Made into tea, the herb was used to settle stomachaches and colic in young children. It was also helpful at the beginning stages of a cold, and because of its pleasant taste children accepted it easily.

Haden was a pediatrician who came from a family with a long tradition of folk healing. Serafina taught cultural anthropology at the University of New Mexico and was the daughter and the granddaughter of *curanderos*. Both Haden and Serafina believed in the efficacy of sympathetic magic.

Not that sympathetic magic was the only kind they practiced.

Among Haden's forebears, there were conjurers as well as healers.

A number of Serafina's aunts were *brujas*.

The Wolfs took a pragmatic approach to life: whatever worked.

Reaching a clearing, Serafina came to an abrupt stop, forcing Haden, who required a greater braking distance, to dodge to his wife's right to avoid a collision. As he came to a halt, Haden raised the carbine to his shoulder. He didn't fire, not yet.

He sensed Serafina creep forward. She laid a hand on her husband's back. If the time came when she thought a shot should be taken, she would give him a pat. Just hard enough to be felt, not so forceful as to disrupt his aim.

Less than ten feet from the couple was a crudely constructed six-foot-high scaffold. Four upright posts with forked tops had been set into the soil. Side poles had been laid into the forks; cross poles had been placed over the side poles. The structure was a crude but effective example of aerial sepulture: committing a person's remains to the sky instead of the earth.

Only the infant on the scaffold, a newborn wrapped in a T-shirt, was far from dead. Its cries rang louder in the Wolfs' ears not only because they were closer now, but because in some fashion the child must have sensed that help was near and this chance for survival was the only one it would have.

Haden and Serafina had to agree.

Pacing back and forth beneath the scaffold, its manner both proprietary and defensive, its growls deeper and more threatening than before, was the largest coyote either of them had ever seen. The animal considered the morsel on the scaffold to be its meal, and was not going to yield it to others without good cause.

The coyote feigned a charge at Haden and Serafina. When they didn't budge, it retreated, resumed pacing under the scaffold, trying to think of a new strategy. The coyote extended its neck, raised its head directly under the infant and howled for all it was worth.

If the big creatures couldn't be frightened into moving, maybe the small creature could.

The baby did react with a sense of increased threat. Its bawling grew in intensity, heightened in pitch. Too young and too constricted by the T-shirt to coordinate any movement resembling flight, it nevertheless began to rock side to side. Even these small efforts made the crude scaffold begin to shake.

The coyote saw what was happening above its head, understood its strategy could succeed, and seemed, to Haden and Serafina, almost to smile. The animal raised its head as if to howl again, hoping to bring its prey within reach. Once that was achieved it would snatch the prize in its jaws and be gone before the slow-footed creatures standing nearby could do anything about it.

Just as the coyote opened its mouth to terrify the child further, a stone hit its snout a stinging blow. The animal's head whipped around to face Haden and Serafina. Magic was all well and good, but there were times when a blunt object thrown with force and accuracy had a more immediate effect, and Serafina had another rock in hand.

Haden had the animal in his sights. Neither he nor Serafina wanted to kill the coyote if it gave them a choice, but if the animal even feigned a charge at them again, it would be met by .44 caliber rounds as well as a rock. For a heartbeat, the beast looked as if it would sacrifice itself for a chance to sink its fangs into one or both of the thieves who sought to steal its meal.

Then reverting to its characteristic wiliness, the coyote pivoted and slammed a shoulder into the nearest upright of the scaffold. The baby shrieked as it felt the platform on which it rested collapse. The Wolfs were already in motion.

Serafina hit the coyote in its hindquarters with the rock she threw, and then she caught the Winchester Haden had lobbed to her. Haden's only college sport had been wrestling, but he dived and stretched out like a wide receiver going for a football in a corner of the end zone. He had his eyes on the baby and he never blinked.

The coyote froze for just a second. The animal saw the meal that should have been its about to fall into its mouth. So close. So ready to be devoured. But approaching at even greater speed was a monstrous creature many times its size, big enough to block out the rising sun. The coyote darted clear before it was crushed.

Haden caught the baby mere inches above the ground. He

rolled to disperse the force of the impact on his body as he cradled the baby to his chest. He glanced over his shoulder and saw the coyote from a worm's-eye view. From that vantage point, the damn thing, not ten yards away, was all snarling teeth and glowing eyes.

The animal, Haden was sure, was about to make one last try for the baby, but then two shots in quick succession kicked up dirt on either side of the animal.

Persuaded now that it was overmatched, the coyote turned and dashed up a nearby brush-covered rise. As it came to the crest it turned to take one last look at the humans now clustered below. Haden had passed the baby to Serafina who cooed into the child's ear.

Haden had taken the Winchester back. He thought the coyote's aggression was spent, but he kept the weapon ready in case he was wrong. For that matter, as far as Haden knew, the coyote wasn't the only predator nearby. He'd brought the carbine along that morning because mountain lions liked to hunt at dawn and dusk.

The coyote seemed almost to be studying the thieves who had stolen its meal, as if to memorize their faces, theirs and that of its lost prey. The animal's anger was clear. If it had had any means to strike back, the fight would not be over.

"Sonofabitch is mad," Haden told Serafina.

The coyote wasn't the only one whose temper was up. Serafina pressed one side of the baby's head to her breast and covered the child's other ear with her hand.

"Show him what happens when we get angry," she said.

Haden snapped off a shot that made the coyote flinch; it must have felt the round pass by. It yelped and disappeared into the brush. Haden and Serafina both admitted later that their mercy toward the coyote might have been misplaced. The wiser choice might have been to kill it.

At the time, though, a more important thought occupied their minds.

"You think the child's mother saw what happened just now?" Haden asked.

Serafina nodded.

Native American women were ones who mourned their dead. The departed, much less those not yet dead, were never simply abandoned.

The Wolfs took the child they'd found, a boy, home.

CHAPTER 2

Austin, Texas — July 8th, the present

It wasn't every day, or any time in the eleven years of life that Amos Blake and his best friend Malachy Sampson had known, that they saw a great big lake, one in which they used to swim and on which they had planned to learn to water ski that summer, just up and disappear. However, that was just what the heck had happened. Lake Travis had about vanished.

There was still some water left. Not enough to wet a fisherman's line, Mal said, much less enough to have any serious fun in. Large sections looked as if someone had planted grass seed in the lake bed and a new prairie was taking over. Other areas, though, were nothing more than large empty stretches of cracked mud. Businesses that had depended on a full, healthy lake had collapsed, as had the market for lakeside homes.

Even so, Amos and Mal, in the spirit of boys their age, saw unrivaled opportunity.

To explore. Because, after all, they were naturally curious.

Their interests in the area of exploration had yet to turn to girls.

"You know what my Uncle Bob dropped in Lake Travis?" Mal asked.

"Your Aunt Dottie," Amos said with a grin.

Mal laughed. His aunt and uncle were always fussing, even when the family went boating, and one time his uncle had tossed his aunt overboard, thinking it might cool her down, though things hadn't worked out that way.

Amos had heard that story about a hundred times from his friend.

"I mean accidentally," Mal said. "It was his football team ring from TCU. He took it off to show my dad it was real gold or something and he dropped it into the lake. He went in right after it, but he never did find it. Maybe now that the lake is dried up we could find it."

Amos thought about that a minute. "I told you my Grandpa Hank came down to Texas from Chicago, right?"

"Because he didn't want to shovel no more fuckin' snow," Mal said, putting on what he imagined to be a Chicago accent. He knew Amos's stories as well as his friend knew his.

"Yeah, but when he was a kid up there he went to see baseball games at the ballpark where the Cubs play. Grandpa said he always made sure he was the last one out of the place after a game. The ushers would get mad and chase him out."

"Why'd he want to stay so long?" Mal knew Amos was going to make a point but he didn't see it yet.

"He told me he stayed because people always dropped or forgot stuff they brought to the game with them. Everything from their wallets to binoculars to a bible."

"A bible?" Mal asked.

"Grandpa said the Cubs needed all the prayers they could get."

That was kinda funny, but more important Mal saw now where Amos was going.

"What you're saying," he told Amos, "is lots of people must've dropped all sorts of stuff off their boats into Lake Travis. Not just my Uncle Bob one time with his ring."

Amos nodded. "Right."

"Your grandpa ever find anything good up there in Chicago?"

"Said he put himself through his first year of college with what he found."

Amos and Mal both grinned.

They were sure their parents would have forbidden them from

exploring the dried lake bed if it had ever occurred to them their sons could be so foolish as to try that, but it hadn't. Amos and Mal set off on their bikes to see what they could find.

What they found was a skeleton sticking up out of the mud.

Amos saw the skull first. That was after they'd found all sorts of trash. The only thing of value they had discovered up to that point was a gold earring with a large blue stone that both boys hoped was an actual gem. Mostly, though, what they'd come across was a bunch of junk. It was disgusting the way people had thrown so much garbage overboard.

So when Amos spotted the skull he thought it had to be plastic.

With a great big crack running down the middle of the forehead.

"Look," he said, pointing it out to Mal, "somebody was playing Halloween out on the lake."

Mal cracked a grin. "Probably some high school guy brought it along to scare his girlfriend, 'Boo!' She got pissed and threw the thing in the water."

Mal's theory held up only until the boys got closer to the skull.

"That thing's real," Amos said, his stomach starting to knot.

"Look," Mal said. "Is that a foot?"

Projecting from a crack in the mud not far from the skull were metatarsal bones.

It was no great feat of imagination for both boys to guess what connected Point A to Point B beneath the mud: the rest of a skeleton. They were scared now — had never expected to find a body — but they were fascinated, too. Had the skeleton once been a kid like them, someone who'd fallen off a boat, drowned and never been found?

The skull proved more worthy of their attention than the foot.

"Wow," Mal said. "I bet this guy's brains leaked right out through that hole in his head."

Amos nodded, and a thought occurred to him: You don't get your head bashed in from drowning. Then he saw something that made him moan. That scared the hell out of Mal.

"What? What's wrong?" Mal's voice was high and tight.

Amos pointed at a loop of rusted metal sticking halfway out of the mud just below the skull. "What's that look like to you?"

Mal had good eyesight but he squinted anyway. "I don't know. What the hell is it?"

"It's a link in a chain."

"You sure?"

Amos said, "I think so. I remember on a trip to Dallas we passed a flatbed truck. It had this big piece of steel on it, held in place by great big chains."

Mal bent over for a closer look. "I think you're right." He knelt on the lake bed and looked up at Amos, "Let's do a little digging and make sure."

Amos yanked his friend to his feet, shook his head and said, "Don't."

"Why not?"

"My dad says not to. You never touch someone who was killed."

"You think this guy was killed?" Mal asked.

Amos gave him a cutting look. "He's got a chain on him. What's that tell you?"

Mal caught on. "He's got a hole in his head, too. That's not good either. You gonna call your dad?"

Amos took out his cell phone and nodded.

"You know our mamas and daddies aren't gonna like us being out here," Mal said.

"I know. But my dad should know about this. He's always tells me, 'When in doubt give me a shout.'"

"Thinking about it now, I ain't got much doubt," Mal said.

"Me either," Amos agreed.

Nonetheless, he called his father, homicide detective Darton Blake of the Austin Police Department.

Darton Blake was at his desk in the homicide unit when he took the call from his son. He listened closely and remained calm.

He told Amos that he and Mal should stay right where they were. They'd done the right thing not to touch anything, and they should continue to stand clear of the body, but they had to keep it in sight. He didn't want to have to go looking for it.

He told Amos to keep his phone on and not to worry. Officers from a patrol unit would be joining him and Mal directly. After a moment of reflection, Darton stayed on the phone with his son until the uniforms got to the scene. They confirmed the presence of skeletal remains and what looked like a link in a chain.

The detective told the patrol officers to stand clear, too. Then he informed Lieutenant Ernie Calderon, the homicide unit's CO of the situation and headed out to Lake Travis. He was accompanied by a crime scene team, and a doc from the Travis County Medical Examiner's Office. Everyone on the scene came to the same conclusion: They had a murder victim on their hands, and they could use additional expert help.

Darton placed a call to the University of Texas and wrangled the help of an archaeologist, a physical anthropologist and a gaggle of grad students. They arrived at the scene, set up a large tent around the remains, set up portable lights inside and positioned three video cameras. With the preliminaries accomplished, they proceeded very carefully to unearth the last vestiges of a human being who had been dumped into Lake Travis.

Lieutenant Calderon put in an appearance to observe the work. At that point, responsibility for the investigation belonged to the Austin PD. Only an hour into the excavation, though, the archaeologist found and bagged a turquoise amulet and a silver chain that had been worn around the neck of the victim. Darton Blake thought the amulet looked like a piece of Native American jewelry, the sort that could be found almost anywhere in the Southwest.

Ernie Calderon stepped in for a look just as Darton turned the plastic bag around to inspect the back of the amulet. Engraved there were the words *Randy Mato Chante*.

The homicide unit's commanding officer wrinkled his brow.

"Randy I kill Chante," Calderon said, as if translating the

words from Spanish.

Darton had another idea. "Native American jewelry, could be a Native American tongue."

"Yeah, could," his boss said. "You handle it. I've got other things to do."

Darton called UT again. Fine school that it was, he reached a research librarian who could help him. After only five minutes of consulting her tomes, or databases as the case may be, she said, "Randy Mato Chante is a name: Randy Bear Heart. I checked on that name, and do you know who that man is?"

Darton didn't tell her she was using the wrong verb tense.

"Sorry to say I don't, ma'am," he replied.

"Well, he isn't a very nice person. In fact, he's a federal fugitive."

And that was how the FBI got involved.

Them and John Tall Wolf.

CHAPTER 3

Austin, Texas — July 9th, the present

S AC Gilbert Melvin and three FBI underlings had flown to
Austin from Washington and were on the scene by the following morning. Four feds from headquarters showing up was
a measure of Randy Bear Heart's significance. In 1985, he had
gone on a brief but bloody rampage robbing three banks, two in
North Dakota one in South Dakota, and killing three cops, with
the same geographical distribution. In addition to those crimes,
he was suspected of kidnapping a woman and a child from the
Mercy Ridge Reservation. He'd been one of the FBI's most wanted
men ever since.

The temperature that morning had already reached 99 degrees
and inside the enclosure, even with the flaps up, the air was a good
ten degrees hotter. The heat didn't move Gilbert or his men to
loosen their ties or drape their suit coats over their arms. Darton
Blake wore a short sleeve shirt, Dockers and Chuck Taylor Low-
Tops.

He'd dressed down for the weather and for the occasion.

The skeleton had been completely, painstakingly uncovered by
the UT team. The doc from the ME's office had defined the hole
in the victim's skull as an edged-surface trauma, but would need
more than an eyeball look to tell whether it was accidental or homicidal. She'd also allowed for the possibility that such a determination
might not be possible if the body had been in the water for a period
measured in years.

The medical examiner wanted to have the remains transported to the county morgue, but Darton thought it would be a good idea to let the feds get a look at the skeleton *in situ.* The ME approved of his Latin if not his decision.

SAC Melvin bent over the remains and asked, "You think the blow to the head killed the guy before he went in the water?"

He hadn't addressed the question to anyone in particular.

His head swiveled when an unfamiliar voice answered, "Maybe, maybe not."

Melvin and the other cops on hand, federal and local, turned to the guy who'd given the ambiguous answer: a big, Indian-looking guy, all lean muscle, neat haircut, wearing a black polo shirt, nicer khakis than the local dick wore and silver-gray aviator sunglasses.

A tall man in Ray-Bans. He was way too big to miss, but he hadn't been in the enclosure a moment ago. Melvin straightened up to eliminate as much of the height difference as he could.

Still came up a half-foot short.

He asked Darton, "This guy one of yours? You kind of dress alike."

The Austin PD detective just shook his head.

"So who the hell are you?" Melvin wanted to know.

The Austin detective was on hand strictly as a courtesy, and his uniformed colleagues outside the enclosure were supposed to keep reporters away. So how'd this big guy get in, and who the hell was he? Someone his size couldn't sneak —

He said, "My name is John Tall Wolf."

So he was an Indian.

"And who said you could join the party, John?" Melvin asked.

"The Great White Father."

Darton Blake cracked a smile, but SAC Melvin didn't like smart-ass from anyone.

He said, "Which great white father would that be?"

"The one with the place on Pennsylvania Avenue."

"The *president* sent you?"

"Through the offices of the agency I work for." John showed his

ID. "I'm a fed, too. BIA."

It took Melvin a moment, then the acronym registered. "Bureau of Indian Affairs?"

"Office of Justice Services," John said. "Of the three cops Randall Bear Heart killed, two were Caucasian, but one was a Native American, a Mercy Ridge Reservation cop. That part of the case is my responsibility."

"Shit," Melvin said.

"A great big pile with a cloud of flies," John agreed.

Melvin hated this development, and he wasn't crazy about the Indian's attitude either. The FBI had been given responsibility for major crimes committed on Indian reservations, but since the 1975 killing of two special agents on the Mercy Ridge Reservation, the Bureau had come to accept the wisdom of letting BIA agents, inevitably Native Americans, carry part of the load. The BIA had authorization to conduct concurrent investigations on reservation related crimes.

Bank robberies, however, were the exclusive domain of the FBI.

So it was time to let the Indian know who was boss.

Melvin told John. "You'll coordinate all your efforts through me."

"I'll conduct my investigation as I see fit," John said.

Before the federal pissing match could go any farther, Darton Blake asked, "Special Agent Tall Wolf, what makes you think Mr. Bear Heart might have been alive when he went into the water?"

John took his eyes off Melvin and looked at the Austin detective.

"I worked a case in Minnesota. Guy was thrown out of a powerboat wearing chains, but he was still conscious. He tried to kick his way to the surface. Almost made it. The bad guys, though, circled back to check their work. The propeller on their boat clipped the victim's head. Did damage that looked a lot like that."

John gestured to the crease in the skeleton's skull.

All the cops present took another look.

It wasn't hard to imagine John might be right.

Melvin, still displeased, said in a snide tone, "Or it could have been a tomahawk made that wound."

John considered the possibility and nodded. "Maybe. Anybody find one?"

Nobody had.

"The case I worked," John continued, "I found the boat before the bad guys could ditch the motor. The damaged propeller blade was a dead-on fit to the wound."

Melvin took a deep breath and let it out slowly. He didn't like competition, but he wasn't dumb enough to overlook a potentially valuable resource. So he choked back a little pride.

He said to John, "How about you liaise with me? That too much to ask?"

John said, "I'll talk with the detective here." He nodded to Darton. "You're nice to him, maybe he'll share with you."

Darton Blake smiled. He'd just been made a relevant member of the team.

The detective said to Melvin, "We casual Friday guys have to stick together."

None of the FBI men sweating up their business suits so much as grinned.

"I can coordinate with the FBI," Darton said to John. "If they're nice to me."

The feds didn't think that was funny either.

But Melvin still managed to nod in agreement and lead his men outside.

Once they'd gone, Darton asked John, "How'd you know I'm a detective."

"I asked your guys outside who was inside. You dress a little different than an FBI agent."

Darton smiled and nodded. "Yeah, I do. So do you. You'll have to pardon me if I don't know the extent of your authority. This is the first time I've ever worked with someone from the BIA. You have any special legal powers I should know about?"

"You know how James Bond has that license to kill?" John asked.

Grinning, feeling something good was coming, Darton said, "Uh-huh."

John told him, "I've got one to take scalps."

CHAPTER 4

Santa Fe, NM — June 26, 1975

The baby boy took in the neonatal formula that Haden Wolf had long ago devised for newborns whose mothers were unable to nurse. It was an organic lactose liquid fortified with vitamins, minerals, iron … and a few herbal derivatives even forward-looking companies were unlikely to catch on to for some time. In addition, though it wasn't a big draw locally, the formula was kosher.

Serafina had dressed the baby in one of her clean T-shirts and given him his first bottle. After consuming every drop, he fell asleep in her arms, utterly relaxed, except for the fact his eyelids were not only closed, they were squeezed shut. She repositioned the baby so his head rested on her shoulder.

"Poor little guy got too much sun in his eyes?" she asked.

Haden nodded. "He would have closed them reflexively, if the coyote hadn't been terrifying him. As it was, he didn't know what to do."

"You think there's any permanent damage?"

"Too soon to say."

But not too soon to feel. Serafina sat on her bed and closed her eyes, let her respiration and heartbeat synch up with that of the baby she held. In moments, their body temperatures meshed. Watching the two of them, Haden saw the boundaries between woman and child blur. Serafina had established a rapport with the infant that all good parents know with their newborns at the closest moments they share.

Only with Serafina, that bond was conscious, detailed and searching.

Haden sat motionless on a chair, content to watch, feeling a sense of peace and joy unlike anything he'd ever experienced. He didn't know how long the moment lasted but at some point he took notice of the baby's eyelids relaxing. A smile formed on the child's tiny lips. A tear appeared at the corner of Serafina's right eyelid a heartbeat before she opened it.

She put the child down on the comforter atop their bed.

They built a barricade of pillows around him.

Haden placed another chair at the foot of the bed and they watched the child sleep. They'd never seen anything so fascinating. Each of them was in perfect health. Neither of them had any concerns about infertility. Still, they'd never entertained the idea of either having their own children or adopting.

They had their work, their studies and each other.

The subject of children had never come up.

Until now.

Never bound by empirical thought or conventional notions, the Wolfs were strong believers in omens. Their choices of how to spend that morning were to gather herbs or to drive down to Albuquerque to visit a friend who was recovering from a car accident. They'd heard that the friend was doing well and felt she would be better off spending quiet time with her husband. For the two of them, gathering herbs would be the right choice.

The activity with the greater benefit.

Which at that moment lay before them sleeping peacefully.

"He's going to be big," Haden said.

"A tall Wolf?" Serafina asked.

Haden smiled at his wife. "It was that good?" he asked.

He referred to her bonding with the child.

"It was true on every level."

"His eyes?"

"No focal damage, but he'll always be sensitive to light."

Haden raised an issue to be considered. "There's only one reason for a mother to abandon a healthy child that way."

Serafina said, "The conception was taboo."

"The child is regarded as a source of shame."

They sat in silence. That anyone should consider a newborn in such a negative way …"

"The mother had to see us save him," Haden said.

"It's all but certain she believes in signs, too."

They both knew what that meant. There would be a fight to keep the child.

The birth mother would inevitably have her regrets.

Haden and Serafina made their preparations for when that day would come.

They named the boy John Tall Wolf.

CHAPTER 5

Austin, Texas — July 9, the present

The question was raised by the commanding officer of the Austin PD Homicide Unit, Lieutenant Ernie Calderon. "If this pile of bones really is Randall Bear Heart, why should anyone give a shit who killed him? Sonofabitch killed three cops, he's dead, good."

Detective Darton Blake and John Tall Wolf were sitting in the lieutenant's office.

Darton said, "I think it's the *if* people are concerned about."

"Even if it is him," John added, "it'd be a good idea to learn how he got to Texas and managed to live under a new identity for the past twenty-seven years. That and what happened to the woman and the child he kidnapped from Mercy Ridge."

Calderon rubbed his chin. "Yeah, that's a good point. And I guess with all the terrorist assholes running loose in the world, it'd be worth knowing how he could live off the radar."

"And we don't want the FBI to have all the fun, do we?" John asked.

Calderon laughed. "Hell, no, can't have that. But —"

"Better the manpower costs come out of the federal budget?" Darton asked.

"Every time possible," Calderon agreed.

"Your modesty is truly impressive, Lieutenant," John said. "Willingly forsaking any glory that might come out of this case."

Calderon snorted. "Glory, huh?"

"Good PR anyway," Darton said.

Blake had that much right, Calderon thought. Good publicity was always welcome.

He'd want his name in the headline. Spelled right, too.

Any managerial cop on the make would.

"Okay, Darton, barring riots, plagues or budget cuts, you can work with Special Agent Tall Wolf. Until I can find a better way to have you make me look good."

The two working cops left the lieutenant's office, crossed the detectives bullpen to Darton's desk and began to read the information John had collected on Randy Bear Heart from the BIA's files. John had printed out the stack earlier that morning.

Randall Bear Heart had been born on the Mercy Ridge Reservation in South Dakota on June 26, 1965, ten years to the day before the shootout that killed two FBI agents who had tailed a suspect in an armed robbery, Tommy Big Crow, to the reservation. The FBI agents were met by a hail of high-powered rifle fire coming from the White Horse Ranch. A BIA marksman later killed the leader of the hostile forces holed up in the ranch's big house. That put an end to the fight but it didn't keep a number of people inside the house from slipping out the back door as the federal forces mounted a frontal assault.

An informant later said that Randall Bear Heart and his parents, George and Nellie, were among those who had fled the big house. Randy, as the boy was called, said he was never there. He was reading in the reservation library at the time of the hostilities. Two librarians vouched for his presence there.

When George and Nellie couldn't be located, Randy was asked where his parents were. He said he didn't know, but they'd both talked of going to California to try to break into the movies. They thought it was time some good-looking Native Americans landed leading roles. George and Nellie, Randy said, thought they'd try to jumpstart their acting careers by seeing if they could take a meeting with Marlon Brando.

The feds thought the kid was fucking with them, but both George and Nellie were exceptionally good-looking people, and the kid was flat-out child star handsome — and Brando openly sympathized with the American Indian Movement. So maybe it wasn't bullshit.

Randy got a good laugh years later when a reporter at the reservation's newspaper — where Randy also worked — told him he'd heard from a famous celebrity biographer that Brando had once refused to let a boatload of feds land on the little island he owned way the hell out in French Polynesia after they told him they were looking for fugitive Indians.

"Why the hell didn't we think of that?" the reporter asked Randy. "Just refuse to let the fuckers come ashore in the first place."

Randy was raised by an aunt and uncle who didn't particularly care for him but surely appreciated the envelope of cash that arrived each month to pay for his support. By anything but reservation standards it wasn't a lot of money, but it came right on schedule, year after year. The feds found out about the surreptitious child support only well after Randy learned of it.

Initially, he'd demanded only a small percentage of the money from his aunt and uncle. As he grew older, though, he upped his share and finally claimed all of it. That was when his uncle kicked him out and ratted him out. Confronted by the FBI, Randy claimed he'd received money only once and as it came in an unmarked envelope he had no idea if his long-missing mother and father had sent it. If there had been more payments, they should check with his uncle. He must have kept them and spent them on himself — serve the old bastard right if the feds set him up to roast slowly over an open fire.

That was when Randy was eighteen, had just graduated at the top of his high school class, and had gotten a job at the *Mercy Ridge Times* to support himself. The editor he'd talked to there had asked what he could do. "Get rid of all the damn spelling errors and mangled grammar," Randy had said. "That and make sure the stories are at least semi-factual."

He was hired as the paper's copy editor and outraged all the reporters with his red pencil and fact checking.

The other reservation demographic Randy drove to distraction was the female population, aged eighteen to forty. By near unanimous consent among that group Randy Bear Heart, *aka* Randy Heart Throb, was the most handsome red man the Great Spirit had ever created. Outside of his job, Randy couldn't be bothered with reservation politics or civil rights for his people. He was busy with the ladies and the white man's popular culture.

In particular, he became obsessed by the movie "Bonnie and Clyde," a print of which had found its way to Mercy Ridge. After the movie had finished its public run, Randy had bought the print and paid a few dollars for private screenings in the wee hours of the night.

He'd sit in the dark, either alone or with a girlfriend of the moment, and imagine himself as Warren Beatty playing Clyde Barrow. He looked at Faye Dunaway and ... well, there weren't any natural blondes on the rez, but there were certainly women who cleaned up nice. Two in particular who did.

Watching the film until the print wore out, Randy developed a more general interest in Depression era outlaws. He came to admire a number of them, but he always came back to Arthur Penn's rendition of Clyde Barrow. He just loved the way Beatty inhabited the role. So he was seriously disappointed when he came across a picture of the real life Clyde. The gangster was a little hillbilly looking guy with jug ears and no upper lip. And the real Bonnie Parker? To say she was homely was being kind about it, and she was so scrawny you had to wonder how she ever hefted that Thompson submachine gun.

The way Randy saw the bigger picture, the rez was stuck in a permanent Depression. So he'd be just as justified going out and robbing banks as any of those hard-time white boys had been ... and in all the years that had passed since the real Bonnie and Clyde had been on their rampage — or even since Penn's movie had been made — bankers had forgotten what a cool bank robber looked like.

These days it was all punks with nylons or Halloween masks over their faces. No-style assholes poking their little handguns at tellers who had every right to think they might get shot by accident as easily as on purpose. Where the hell was the cool old-time robber with a sense of fashion? For that matter, was there any robber who looked every bit as good as a movie star?

That thought put Randy in mind of his parents. George and Nellie had looked great. He'd missed them after they'd first run off. He understood that they'd had to leave him behind; they might have gotten caught if they'd been busy worrying about him. They could have gone to prison and … he might have wound up somewhere worse than living with his aunt and uncle.

He still wondered what had happened to his parents, though. They must have done something to make the money they'd sent back to the rez all those years. And somehow, after his uncle had ratted him out to the feds, they'd known to stop the payments. Not give the feds anything to work with. So you could be an outlaw and outsmart the guys with the badges.

In the case of George and Nellie, you'd probably look cool doing it, too.

Randy figured what he ought to do was follow in the traditions of both Arthur Penn and Mom and Dad. He bought himself a lightly used navy blue double-breasted suit and a pearl gray fedora. As a contemporary grace note, he added a pair of cool shades. But, growing impatient, he started robbing banks before he could find a pair of spats.

At the end of the Bear Heart file, John found mention of one of Randy's favorite girlfriends. Her name was Annie Forger. She lived in Rapid City, South Dakota.

John left Darton to pursue the investigation in Austin.

He headed out to Rapid City.

CHAPTER 6

Rapid City, South Dakota — July 10, the present

"Randy was all kinds of smart and more kinds of crazy," Annie Forger told John.

The woman had informed him upon meeting that you used the French pronunciation for her last name: Forzhay. John had studied French in college and could manage that. The two of them were seated in a booth at a 50s-themed diner called Arnold's. Annie told John that her ticket out of the rez was getting the grades to be admitted to the University of North Dakota.

While she was there, she met and fell in love with Vern Forger, the star center of the Fighting Sioux ice hockey team.

"Emigré from Quebec?" John asked.

"*Mais oui,*" Annie said. "French dad, Mohawk mom. Poor Vern lost them both to heart attacks, within a year of each other. He said he thought with his dad it was more of a broken heart than anything else."

John told her, "You'll have to excuse me, but I don't follow hockey. How'd Vern do?"

She gave him a smile and shook her head. "I don't know how you could pick up the sports section of any paper and not have heard of Vern. He went pro with Vancouver. Was an all star his rookie year."

"Well, that's good."

"He gave me two beautiful sons."

"That's even better, but you sound like … are you divorced?"

"Vern died."

John said, "I'm very sorry.

"So was I, but that was quite a while ago."

"Was it another heart problem that took him?" John knew that some young athletes discovered heart anomalies only by dropping dead from them. And if there was a family history…

"No, it was a car wreck. Vern and the team were in L.A. for a game. They won and afterward he and his line-mates went out to celebrate. The guy who was the designated driver hadn't understood that not drinking also meant you weren't supposed to smoke any dope either."

"That's terrible," John said.

Annie took a deep breath and let it out slowly. "It was hard enough to lose the man you love. It was worse telling the boys. They couldn't believe that Daddy wouldn't be coming home. Simply *refused* to believe it for quite a while."

"So you came back home?" John asked.

Annie Forger gave him a hard look. "I'm never going back to the rez."

"But South Dakota?"

"Vern left me with a beautiful house in Vancouver and three million dollars from the life insurance. I thought the money would last longer here. There'd be a nice amount to leave the boys."

"Did it help them, coming here?"

Annie laughed without humor. "They hated it. Wanted to be back in Vancouver playing hockey like Dad. But things worked out. They both earned college hockey scholarships. Guy's at Boston College; Louie's at the University of Maine."

John turned the conversation back to Randall Bear Heart.

"How did Randy show his smarts?"

"We both worked at the *Mercy Ridge Times*. I was a gofer and obit writer saving for college; Randy was the copy editor. He said I was the only one at the paper besides him who could spell worth a damn. He could also spot whenever a reporter was BS-ing. Randy could fact check like he had Google before there was a Google."

Annie smiled at the memory.

"You and he …" John left the thought unfinished.

"Yeah. Randy and me and just about every other pretty girl on the rez."

"Couldn't be many others as pretty as you."

John figured Annie Forger had to be mid-to-late forties, but she looked ten years younger. Her skin was smooth and unblemished, her smile white and even and her jet black hair had a stylish cut that surprised John. Or maybe played to his prejudices. He wouldn't have thought a look like that could be found in Rapid City.

"Are you a rich man, Special Agent Tall Wolf?"

"In every way except money."

Annie laughed. "You drink?"

"Not alcohol."

"Smoke dope when you should be driving sober?"

John shook his head.

"My mom's a *curandera*, among other things. She told me if I ever wanted to get high she'd give me some good stuff. Not classified illegal. Known only to a few. Wouldn't scramble my brain, kill my liver or leave me dying for more."

"Damn," Annie said. "She's got something like that, she ought to bottle it. You would be rich."

John said, "It's not that I don't trust Mom, but it seems to me there ought to be a price for feeling good. Hard work, money, a hangover … something. I never took her up on her offer."

"You're happy being who you are?"

"More often than not." John sipped his orange juice. "So how many serious rivals did you have for Randy's affections, one or two?"

"One. Lily White Bird."

John frowned, remembered the file he'd read on Randy Bear Heart the day before.

"Wasn't that the woman he kidnapped?"

Annie shook her head. "Randy never kidnapped anyone. Lily loved Randy's craziness. I said goodbye to him when he showed me the Tommy gun he'd bought. There were all sorts of guns on the rez, but normal ones, you know. Rifles, shotguns, pistols. Randy was the only one with an old-fashioned gangster machine gun. He thought he was Warren Beatty."

"The actor?"

"The one who played Clyde Barrow."

She leafed through her wallet, took out a photo and slid it over to John

He saw Randy Bear Heart decked out like a 1930s gangster. The description of him in the police reports was "a dude with a big fucking gun." Probably weren't a lot of cinema fans among small-town bank employees in the Dakotas back in those days. Standing next to Randy wearing a beret and a blonde wig was …

"Is that you?" John asked Annie.

She nodded. "I didn't mind a little dress up. But when Randy showed up later with the Tommy gun and wanted us to take a picture with it, I said no. Lily said okay."

"How do you know that?"

Annie dug in her purse and pulled out a photostat of another picture, this one eight by ten. It featured the same Bonnie and Clyde motif, but this time the gun was in the picture, as was a different girl playing Bonnie. She wore the beret and the wig, and both she and Randy had their hands on the weapon.

The second girl was just a bit prettier than Annie. Maybe. Depending on your taste.

Annie said, "We took the pictures in the newspaper offices, after the grownups had gone home. You can keep the copy of that picture if you want." She took her wallet-sized picture back.

"Both of the photos were taken before Randy started robbing banks?" John asked.

Annie nodded. "They were, but I had a bad feeling once I saw that gun. I didn't want to be part of anything that happened. Randy was smart but I was the one going to college."

"Wise choice," John said.

"You going to come back to Rapid City again?" Annie asked.

John said, "Don't think so. Why do you ask?"

Annie shrugged. "I might remember something else to tell you."

"If you do," John said. He gave her his business card.

Annie took it, read it and nodded.

Decided she had one more thing to tell John.

"There's this rumor about Randy. Word was he got away with maybe thirty-five thousand dollars total from his bank jobs. That wasn't bad money back then. It's still more than most people on any rez ever saw before the casinos started opening. But there were whispers Randy stole something a lot more important than money. Not from the banks, from the rez."

John asked, "What?"

"A ghost shirt and a peace pipe. Maybe other sacred items."

John knew if there was one sure way, anywhere in the world, to cause bloodshed it was to disrespect the beliefs other people held as holy. Randy Bear Heart, if the rumors Annie Forger had heard were true, had trampled on the beliefs of his tribe.

He said, "Damn, would he really do that?"

"I told you right off Randy was crazy," Annie said.

CHAPTER 7

Austin, Texas — July 10, the present

SAC Melvin sat in the office he'd been lent in the Austin federal building, skimming the initial medical reports on the remains found in the dry bed of Lake Travis. The distribution list for the material also included John Tall Wolf and Darton Blake, but all paperwork relevant to the case was routed through him. He was the one to decide what information the other two received.

In a world where terrorists had climbed to the top of the Bureau's most wanted list, a small time bank robber who had vanished decades ago was far from a priority. Truth was, the assignment was a none too subtle slap at Melvin. He'd been given the job because he wouldn't be missed elsewhere, not having him work an important case was a good use of resources.

Bastards.

Might as well have told him to retire the first day he was eligible; there wouldn't be any point in sticking around. Certainly no promotion. Maybe he could find a second career as an assistant VP of security at Walmart. Get himself a nice employee discount.

Fuckers.

Melvin's laptop chimed. He had mail.

John Tall Wolf had sent a message, a one-paragraph summary of his interview with Annie Forger. What stuck out for Melvin was the rumor that Bear Heart might have been stealing from other Indians. A ghost shirt, whatever that was, and a peace pipe, which Melvin had always thought was something invented by Hollywood. Neither item meant a thing to him. Not that his opinion was important. It was how the Indians felt that mattered.

Melvin sensed a new opportunity here. He was already counting on some good publicity for closing a case that would bring comfort to relatives of the dead cops. Now, in these ethnically sensitive times, if he could restore some cultural trinkets to the Indians, that should be worth some good ink and airtime, too. Maybe, with a bit of luck, he could return a headdress to a chief. That'd make a cool picture.

You gave Gil Melvin a sack of fertilizer, he'd hand you a bouquet of roses.

Unless, of course, credit went to Tall Wolf.

That big SOB with his sunglasses had made it plain he wasn't going to knuckle under. Given he was an Indian, too, Tall Wolf had to have a better understanding of Bear Heart and the significance of the things he'd stolen from his tribe. If Melvin had to go back to Washington with his tail between his legs and Tall Wolf the hero, he was done.

Done in by a *BIA* agent.

He'd be a joke.

He ate his gun, he'd hear the laughter over the shot that killed him.

So failure was not an option. The thing to do was … well, he'd already recognized that Tall Wolf was no dummy. And he recognized that Tall Wolf had an insider's edge on the Indian angle. The way to play it, then, was to show the guy some grudging respect. Let that become collegial acceptance. Maybe even drop a hint or two of camaraderie. Get him looking the other way.

Then swoop in and grab all the credit.

Melvin wrote a reply to Tall Wolf, thanking him for his information. Telling him he'd received the first of the medical reports. Did Tall Wolf want them emailed to him? Or did he want to read them when he got back to Austin?

He revised that to: The reports were available upon request.

Wouldn't want Tall Wolf to smell a rat.

CHAPTER 8

Santa Fe, NM — June 27, 1975

Haden and Serafina decided to sleep on the matter. See if they weren't being rash about choosing to become parents. After all, it wasn't every day you saved an infant from a wild animal. In a situation that dramatic, maybe wanting to keep the child was just a reflex. When they awoke, however, their minds remained unchanged. They were going to keep the baby. They would keep the name John Tall Wolf, too. Anglo on each end with a Native American ring to it nonetheless. Haden suggested they could add a Latino name to round it out, but Serafina said that wasn't necessary.

They would use a Spanish word for the child's secret name.

The one that would keep him safe from those who might wish to curse him.

The Wolfs knew they would also have to take more mundane precautions to retain custody of John. The law would have to be served. They couldn't simply keep the boy. They called their lawyer; he called a judge. The judge brought in an outside pediatrician and the police.

The cops listened to the Wolfs' story and went out with Haden and found the remnants of the platform on which John had been abandoned. They saw the coyote's footprints all around the fallen structure. They smelled the animal's urine, understood that it had staked its claim. All others had better stay away.

Everything was photographed. Traps were set for the coyote, should it return.

The beast was never caught.

The pediatrician brought in by the judge pronounced John to be in good health, though the child winced and cried when she shined a light on his eyes. The doctor said it was clear to her that the child was already bonding with the Wolfs. Once she finished with her official duties, she asked if she might have a sample of Haden's baby formula.

The judge decided it was in the best interest of the child that he remain with the Wolfs as they had declared their intention to adopt him. Their custody would be considered temporary for ninety days to give one or both biological parents the opportunity to reassert their parental rights to the child.

The last thing the Wolfs wanted was for the fool or fools who had imperiled John to pop up at the last minute and stake their claim. So they took the initiative. They paid to have ads placed in Anglo, Native American and Latino publications that a baby boy had been found. They gave the details and asked anyone knowing anything about the child to come forward and contact the authorities. As more than a few people in the area weren't the best readers, the announcement was also broadcast by radio stations serving all segments of the community.

Haden and Serafina felt certain John's birth mother wouldn't come forward, but they weren't sure what the biological father might do if he learned he had a son. Watching John thrive day by day, holding him, feeding him, reading stories to him, they felt the child take possession of their hearts. At some level, John knew that Haden and Serafina had saved his life, and he put his complete trust in them.

Those first three months they spent together were the most joyous and the most anxious of the Wolfs' lives.

They were weak with relief when the deadline passed and no one had come forward to claim John. Pursuant to the judge's order, Dr. and Mrs. Haden Wolf were allowed to adopt the male infant to be known as John Tall Wolf.

***

The child's biological mother, Bly Black Knife, a member of the Northern Apache nation, had heard the announcement about her son broadcast on the reservation's radio station, but she didn't dare bring shame on her parents. She was also not going to arouse Coyote's wrath.

Six years later, though, after her father had died, she changed her mind.

A suit was filed to set aside the Wolfs' adoption.

CHAPTER 9

Austin, Texas — July 11, the present

John lowered himself onto the visitor's chair next to Darton Blake's desk in the bullpen of the homicide unit of the Austin Police Department.

"Nice to see you again, Special Agent," Darton said. "Take any scalps lately?"

"Haven't had the need. Your son turn up any more skeletal fugitives?"

Blake laughed. "Not a one. I've strongly cautioned Amos about that."

John took out the eight-by-ten copy of the photograph of Randy Bear Heart and Lily White Bird doing their Bonnie and Clyde impressions. He slid it over to the detective.

"Sorry about the fuzziness," John said, "but that's what we have to work with. What you see there is Mr. Bear Heart when he still had some flesh on him. The woman with him is Lily White Bird, aka Mrs. Daniel Red Hawk."

Darton looked up from the grainy image. "The woman Bear Heart kidnapped?"

"We'll have to revise our thinking on that. Annie Forger told me kidnapping wasn't in Bear Heart's criminal repertoire. What I heard, Lily was Randy's favorite girlfriend, and her little boy, name of Jackson, was really Randy's son, not the late Officer Red Hawk's."

"Well, ain't that a kick in the head?" Darton asked, looking at John.

"Yeah. Especially if you were Red Hawk. Try looking past the beret and the blonde wig. See if you can recall ever seeing Lily around Austin. I don't figure Randy for taking her off the rez only to leave her at a bus stop somewhere."

The detective put his eyes back on the photostat. "No, sir. You wouldn't leave a looker like this behind even if ..."

John asked, "A thought cross your mind, Detective?"

"I was gonna say you wouldn't leave her even if she was poisoning your popcorn. Then it occurred to me maybe somebody slipped old Randy a mickey. Knocked him out long enough to get all those chains around him."

John nodded, liked the idea. "Weigh him down then wake him up when he's in the boat. Let him see what he's got coming."

"Sure," Darton agreed. "The fun part is where he begs for mercy or just plain soils himself. I'll have to ask the lab boys if poison might linger in the bone marrow or somewhere else."

"I know it shows up in hair follicles, but I don't remember seeing any hair on the skull."

"Me either, but maybe on the part in back that was stuck in the mud. I'll ask."

"Try to jog your memory about Lily, too," John said.

"I'm working on that already. Thing is, it's not likely she's blonde and she's got to be, what, twenty-some years older. She might look a whole lot different."

John said, "Some women hardly age at all. Others do it very well."

His mother for one.

Darton looked like he had something to add, but he was beaten to the punch.

"What an enlightened attitude," a female voice said.

The two men turned their heads and saw a woman in a business suit. Tall, sleek and striking. A streak of white running through long black hair. Darton turned back to John.

"Gotta be one of yours," he said. "We don't have any like her."

"My boss," John said.

CHAPTER 10

Mercy Ridge Reservation, South Dakota — August 20, 1986

R andy "Clyde" Bear Heart's favorite "Bonnie" was Lily White Bird. Not only was she the prettiest girl on the rez, she had moments when she was damn near as crazy as he was. Not that Randy thought of himself as a loon; he fashioned himself as a social activist who made the most of the second amendment. An entrepreneur who believed in taking from the rich and investing in himself. Young people with ambition were natural self-publicists.

Lily had not only posed with Randy's Tommy gun, she'd fired it. At her insistence, the two of them and little Jackson had gone off to a remote area of the rez and, after stopping up the baby's ears with cotton, Lily had fired off a whole drum of ammo. The experience got her so worked up that she and Randy lay down on the blanket they'd brought with them and had at it not two feet from the still smoking weapon.

Lily was the only girl Randy had sex with when he wasn't wearing protection.

That decision carried with it more than the usual risks, as Lily was married to a reservation cop. If word got out what Randy was doing, it wouldn't be only Daniel Red Hawk who came looking for him. All the cop's friends with badges would be in the posse. Randy had cut a wide swath through the women on the rez, and most of the men thought none too highly of him.

He was too smart, too good looking and too much competition for their girlfriends and, as with Lily White Bird, sometimes their wives. If Red Hawk and his friends found proof that Randy had gone too far with Lily, he might die resisting arrest. With plenty of corroborating testimony that Randy had been reaching for an officer's weapon.

It turned out that the father, not a husband or boyfriend, of one of Randy's lesser Bonnies almost did him in. He'd found a picture of his daughter and Randy in costume. He knew about Randy's reputation as a ladies' man from all the stories going around the rez. It wasn't hard to imagine the prick was doing more than playing dress up with his daughter. So after the second bank robbery, the one in North Dakota, the angry father had no trouble identifying the culprit after hearing the bank robber's description: a dude with a big fucking gun.

Actually, he'd heard the unedited description.

A fucking *Indian* dude with a big fucking gun.

Someone else might have fingered Randy sooner if the need to be politically correct hadn't rendered the media description less specific. As it was, the father saw the opportunity to rid his daughter of a boyfriend he didn't want around. He called the reservation cops and ratted out Randy.

That might have been the end of the story if the lesser Bonnie hadn't overheard her father's call to the cops and *ratted* him out to Randy, giving the outlaw just enough time to avoid arrest. The smart thing for Randy to do would have been simply to run, but he stopped at the Red Hawk house to pick up his best Bonnie and his son.

He had no intention of killing Daniel Red Hawk. The only reason he'd shot the two cops outside the banks he'd robbed was they had shot at him first. They had died and he'd lived because small-town cops carried .38s not Tommy guns. The way Randy saw it, he'd acted in self-defense, and you couldn't blame him for being better prepared.

Still, there were some things you just couldn't anticipate. Like a rez cop who *always* stopped off after his shift to get shitfaced deciding that he would come straight home that day and try to get his marriage back on the rails. It had finally occurred to Daniel Red Hawk that maybe the reason he couldn't perform in bed with his beautiful wife was that he always got lubed before he got home.

That day, Red Hawk thought things might be a lot more interesting if he could get a few drinks in both of them.

For Lily's part, the only reason she'd married Red Hawk was that she'd had a big argument with Randy. About him screwing other girls, of course. She hadn't seen the humor when he told her she was the only Bonnie who got his best efforts. She scratched his cheek bloody.

In return, he raised a hand to her, but as angry as he was he couldn't follow through with the blow. He just turned and walked out without saying a word. Many were the times Lily wished he had hit her. For one thing, she deserved it. For another, it might have saved her from a moment of true madness. Deciding to marry Daniel Red Hawk.

She'd thought marrying such an oaf would wound Randy's ego.

That she could even pretend to love Red Hawk, and to live with him, would be an insult unlike any other Randy had ever suffered. All the other Bonnies would think Lily was crazy, but if she had thrown Randy over for Red Hawk … maybe it was possible she knew something about him that they didn't.

What they didn't know was how much she loathed living with her husband. How she made him wear a condom any time — and there weren't many — she let him have her. Daniel Red Hawk couldn't help but see his wife's disdain for him, but there was no way he wanted to let so beautiful a woman go. So he adapted to prevailing conditions. Never a teetotaler before he married Lily, Red Hawk's drinking increased steadily afterward.

Lily made her own adjustments. Her anger at Randy changed to regret. How could she have damaged that perfect face? If she had scarred him, she would have to kill herself. There was no other suitable punishment for destroying such beauty. Then again, troubled eighteen year old girls tended to make dramatic judgments.

Much to Lily's surprise, Randy sent her a note of apology.

Paid an old illiterate woman to deliver it, so their secret would be safe.

Randy said, *"I am who I am, but I shouldn't have made fun about us. Sorry."*

Illiterate courier or not, Randy had neither addressed the note to Lily nor signed it. He'd typed it, too. Had the reservation's cops possessed the wherewithal to match the note to the typewriter, they would have found the machine belonged to them. As part of his job for the *Mercy Ridge Times,* Randy picked up items from the cops for the police blotter column.

The officer responsible for delivering the content of the column had been in the john when Randy arrived. Making himself at home, sitting at the officer's desk, Randy looked at the typewriter in front of him and was inspired to write his apology. He knew how to touch type, but he used only two fingers. Anybody hearing rapid-fire *clickety-click* typing would have gotten suspicious. *Peck, peck, peck* was the usual order of things.

As it was, nobody ever found out.

The apology was all Lily needed to forgive Randy.

He hadn't promised to reform anything but his manners, but that was enough.

After Lily found out she was pregnant with Randy's child, she let Daniel Red Hawk have her one time unsheathed. She told him she wanted to have a child, but he would get only one chance so he better make it good. That night, Lily did have a couple of drinks in her.

Three years later, when Randy finally came to take her away from the rez, he was sitting on her old suitcase so she could snap it shut when Daniel Red Hawk came home. Randy was looking the wrong way when the man of the house entered his bedroom. But Lily knew just what to do.

She took the house gun that Red Hawk kept on the table next to the bed and shot him with it.

Jackson, who'd been asleep on the bed, woke up crying.

Randy took the gun from her hand and said, "Anyone asks,

chalk this one up to me."

What the hell? He had two dead cops to his name already.

Before absconding with Lily and Jackson, Randy had paid a call on the tribal cultural center, the back room where they kept the good stuff white eyes never got to see. Tying up and gagging the elderly couple who oversaw the maintenance of historical relics, he stole a ghost shirt and two peace pipes. There was a war lance he wanted to take, but it was too big to hide.

Having been betrayed already by his aunt and uncle and one of his Bonnies' father, he wanted to leave the tribe with something to think about.

He told the old couple, "Nobody from the tribe rats me out, all this stuff will be returned in perfect condition ... but only after I die a *natural* death."

CHAPTER 11

Santa Fe, New Mexico — September 9, 1981

The suit to determine who should have custody of the child known as John T. Wolf was heard in the Children's Division of the Circuit Court of Santa Fe County. It pitted two families and two communities against each other. The Anglo and Native American residents divided neatly along ethnic lines — even though Serafina, an American by birth, had parentage that was both Mexican and indio.

The families represented by two of the most prominent names in their constituencies, the Wolfs and the Black Knifes. Haden and Serafina were prominent professionals. The Wolfs also contributed to the commonweal with Haden providing free medical care to the indigent three days per week, while Serafina taught adult literacy classes. The Black Knifes were the family of the late Cesar Black Knife, the senior member of the tribal council and the top advisor to the tribal president. The family was active as advocates for the civil rights of Native Americans.

All this was in the mind of the judge hearing the case, Emilio Marquez. He drew the case as each side had Hispanic heritage and he was thought likely to be the most impartial jurist available.

When Perico Fuentes, the lawyer for the biological mother, Bly Black Knife, asked to have a psychologist hired by the tribe talk to the child without the Wolfs being present, Angeline Legget, the Wolfs' lawyer, objected. But Haden and Serafina agreed, if Ms. Legget and the judge were also present and the conversation was recorded on video.

By the judge's decision, six-year-old John would have to answer only four of the several dozen questions the plaintiff's psychologist, Dr. Naomi Winsted, had wanted to ask, and he would be the one to direct the questions to the child. Only the judge, the two lawyers, Dr. Winsted and the video camera operator would be allowed in the room with John.

The judge would be the only one to speak to the child.

If either lawyer had a point to make, he or she would address the judge.

Briefly. After raising his or her hand.

With the ground rules set and everyone in place, Judge Marquez asked that John be brought into his chambers. The boy appeared dressed in a suit, his tie neatly knotted, his shoes shined. He wore tinted glasses. He walked directly over to the judge, sat in the chair to which the judge gestured and ignored the others.

"Good morning, young man," Judge Marquez said.

"Good morning, sir," John replied.

"Do you know who I am?"

"Yes, sir. I was told. You're the judge."

"That's right." Marquez took note of John's glasses. "Do you have trouble with your eyes, John?"

"Bright lights make me squint. Real bright lights make my eyes sting. Unless I wear my glasses."

"But you can see things clearly?"

"Yes, sir."

The judge moved on to the matter at hand. "John, I'm going to ask you four questions. I think they should all be easy for you to answer. Is that all right with you?"

"Yes, sir."

"John, who is your mother?"

"Serafina Wolf y Padilla," the boy answered.

Emilio Marquez kept a straight face but it warmed his heart that the child included his mother's Hispanic surname, and used the proper form of address. Kid's accent wasn't bad either.

"Who is your father, John?"

"Haden Erik Wolf."

John had delivered the first answer seriously. Now, he began to get suspicious. These questions were too easy. There had to be a trick coming.

"Do you love your mother and father, John?"

"Yes."

Another easy one. Now, John was sure a trap was being set.

Judge Marquez asked the fourth question. "Other than being with your mother and father, is there anywhere else you would rather live?"

There it was, the trap. John jumped out of his seat and yelled, "No!"

Marquez remained calm. "Thank you, John. You may —"

Perico Fuentes raised his hand; the Native American lawyer wanted to prolong the matter.

"Yes, Mr. Fuentes?" the judge asked.

"Your Honor, may I please ask John just one question?"

John stood his ground and looked at the man. He shook off the hand Angeline Legget put on his shoulder. The judge noticed the child's courage. He beckoned Fuentes.

"For my ears only, Mr. Fuentes," the judge told the lawyer.

He listened and turned to the boy standing in front of him.

"John," the judge said, "I have one last question. You may choose to answer it or refuse to answer it. It's your choice and whatever you choose is okay with me. Do you understand?"

John nodded.

"Very well. John, will you please tell us what the T in your name, John T. Wolf, stands for?"

John smiled, stood as straight as he could and said, "Tall."

Perico Fuentes had been hoping John's middle name was Thor.

Or Trygve. Something a Norse father with the middle name of Erik might give a son. Something that might be used to show that the Wolfs were denying the child any sign of his ethnic and cultural heritage. But using Tall along with the family surname of Wolf was quite clever. Tall Wolf approximated a Native American name even if that wasn't its intent.

In most instances, Fuentes, like any other good lawyer, wouldn't have asked a question to which he didn't know the answer. In this case he took a chance and lost, but not in front of a jury. So be it. He still had a winning hole card to play.

In his opening statement, Fuentes stood before the jury and said, "There is no claim to parental custody greater than that of a biological mother, and that claim is doubly significant when it is asserted by a member of a Native American tribe whose numbers have been reduced to a small fraction of what they had been at their peak. That diminished number is still threatened by the former depredations and current neglect of the federal government. The government and those people who arrived in this land thousands of years after its original inhabitants. I think you'll understand that these dire circumstances add to the urgency of returning John Tall Wolf to the woman who gave him life."

As the trial proceeded, Fuentes put Bly Black Knife on the stand because he had no choice. A woman couldn't expect a jury to award her custody of a child if she refused to make a case for her claim. Bly had to tell the jury that she'd loved her child even before he was born, a claim no one else could make. She had to make that claim in her own words, and explain the confusion and emotional torment that led her to abandon him.

"Ms. Black Knife," Fuentes asked, "how old were you when you gave birth to the child known as John Tall Wolf?"

"Eighteen."

"Had you finished high school at the time?"

"No."

"Did you have any plans for your future?"

Bly shook her head. "No."

Fuentes asked, "Did anyone else have plans for you?"

"My father did."

"Cesar Black Knife was your father?"

"Yes."

"Your father was the senior member of the Northern Apache tribal council?"

"Yes."

"Do you know what your father's plan for you was?" Fuentes asked.

"To make a good match for me."

"An arranged marriage?"

"A marriage with political benefits."

In the gallery, Bly's mother, Maria Black Knife wore a mask of unflinching disapproval as she looked at her daughter. That Bly should have brought the family to this public humiliation was nothing less than a disgrace. Despite her disapproval, Maria was, by far, more compassionate than her late husband would have been.

"Would this have been a marriage without love?" Fuentes asked.

Up to that point, Fuentes had instructed his client to give simple, factual answers.

The question about love was the cue to let her emotions show.

Bly said, "For me, it wouldn't have been a marriage at all."

"Did you tell your mother and father how you felt?"

She shook her head. "You didn't tell my father anything; he told you."

"Were you afraid of your father?"

Bly's chin began to quiver. "Yes."

Sitting next to Maria Black Knife was Bly's brother, also named Cesar. He knew his sister's fear of their father was well founded. He thought, though, she should have known enough to be afraid of him, too. She should have kept her mouth shut about the kid and the family's shame hidden.

Fuentes asked, "When would you have been expected to marry to suit your father's purposes?"

Bly's fear was replaced by a look of contempt.

"Before I turned nineteen. My father had two suitors in mind for me; he had to decide which of them would bring a greater return."

"You saw no way out of your predicament?"

"I thought of killing myself," Bly said.

Both her mother and brother had to refrain from nodding, thinking that would have been the preferable course.

"Obviously, you thought not to do that," Fuentes said. "So what did you do?"

"I decided to disgrace myself, so no man in our tribe would want me."

"How did you do that?" Fuentes asked softly.

Bly gathered the strength to look directly at the lawyer and answer, "By giving myself to a man not of our tribe, and that's what I did."

"A white man?"

"No."

"A Latino?"

"No."

That was an important point, as Fuentes would make clear in his closing argument.

Bly Black Knife had strayed from her tribe but only so far.

She wouldn't give herself to a man who wasn't a Native American.

Wouldn't want her child to be raised outside the People.

"Did you think you would become pregnant?" Fuentes asked.

Tears welled in Bly's eyes. "I didn't think you could. Not just from one time."

"Would your father have accepted your child had you told him of your pregnancy?"

Bly shook her head. "No."

"Your mother?"

"She obeyed my father, always."

"Other family, friends or simply people of good will?"

Bly's face became as bitter as her mother's. "For anyone else, of course. At the cost of angering Cesar Black Knife, no."

"So what did you do?" Fuentes asked.

The bitterness dropped away from Bly's face, leaving nothing behind.

She spoke in a flat voice. "I met a smiling boy at a rodeo. He was the one. All I knew of him was that his first name was Billy. I had no way of finding him when I became pregnant. I was alone and terrified. I didn't tell anyone. I dressed so no one could see my condition."

"If no one knew you were pregnant, why didn't your father try to go through with his plans for you?" Fuentes asked.

"I don't think anyone knew about the baby," Bly said. She lowered her eyes. "But everyone could see I wasn't the same. I wasn't pretty anymore. I didn't laugh. I barely spoke. No one would want me. If I were smarter, I would have thought of doing that before I met Billy."

With the judge's permission, Fuentes gave Bly his handkerchief to dry her eyes.

She continued, "By the time my son came, I had made the preparations to offer him to the Great Spirit. I prayed that he would be taken quickly and without pain."

"But that wasn't what happened, was it?" Fuentes asked.

"No."

"What do you want now?"

John wasn't in the courtroom, but Haden and Serafina were.

Bly looked right at them and said, "I want my son back."

Angeline Legget began her cross-examination by coming straight to the point.

"Other than the Great Spirit, Ms. Black Knife, who deserves credit for John's survival, his health and his general well being?"

"They do," Bly said without looked at Haden and Serafina.

"You mean Dr. and Mrs. Wolf?"

"Yes, them."

"Have you received through your attorney, Mr. Fuentes, the court's assessment of exactly how well John is doing?"

"I've seen the report."

"Good. Can you tell me then if you could have done better?"

Bly Black Knife couldn't cry poor because her family wasn't poor, not by the standards of their people. But there was that other problem.

"I couldn't have brought my son home because of my father," Bly said.

"So, the answer is no, even if you had kept John, you couldn't have done as well by him."

Bly's face tightened in anger. "Not because I wouldn't have wanted to."

Legget nodded, a thoughtful expression on her face.

"Let's take a look at that notion. In response to Mr. Fuentes' question, you said that nobody on your tribal lands would have taken John in for fear of angering your father. Is that right?"

"Yes."

"Well, then, since you came quite close to Santa Fe, leaving tribal land, to tender John to the mercies of the Great Spirit, why not go just a bit farther and leave him, say, at a fire station or a hospital or a church? Someplace where you could count on a responsible adult to take him into safekeeping. Somewhere a coyote would be less likely to make a meal of your newborn child."

Fuentes objected; the judged sustained the objection. But the point had been made.

Tears flowed from Bly's eyes. She still had Fuentes' handkerchief, but didn't move to stem the flow. She said, "I don't know."

Angeline Legget was sure Bly knew, but that was all right. The true answer to that question was the ace up *her* sleeve.

"Ms. Black Knife, if your father were still alive, would you be in court now asking for custody of John?"

Bly hung her head. "No."

"Wanting John back then is what, just a matter of circumstance?"

Bly's head snapped up. "I thought about killing my father. I thought about it many times."

A woman with homicidal notions wanted custody of a child? That should have been the ball game right there, Angeline thought.

But juries often produced confounding results.

The Wolfs' lawyer kept going. "We're all grateful there's no other heartbreak for a court to consider. Now, Ms. Black Knife, on the morning you commended John into the keeping of the Great Spirit, did you wait nearby to see if your hope would be realized?"

"Yes."

"Will you please tell the jury what happened while you were watching?"

"The sun came up."

Legget nodded. "Making it easier for you to see what happened next."

Knowing she had no way to evade, Bly said, "Coyote came."

Not a coyote, Legget thought. Coyote with a capital C. Good lawyer that she was, Legget wasn't about to let herself be diverted down a trail of mythology.

"This coyote, did it just come and go, showing no interest in John?"

"No."

"It came and it stayed?"

"Yes."

"Did the animal show any awareness of John's presence?"

"I don't know what you mean."

Legget said, "Did it sniff, did it howl, did it growl, did it pee to mark its turf?"

"Objection. Compound question," Fuentes said.

"Break it down, please, Ms. Legget," the judge instructed.

She did and Bly was forced to admit the coyote did all the things Legget had enumerated.

"Did any of these actions strike you as threatening, Ms. Black Knife?"

Bly waited long enough for the judge to prompt her to answer. "Yes," she said.

"Did you think it was the Great Spirit's intention to have a coyote eat your child, Ms. Black Knife?"

"No!"

"Were you afraid to intervene on your child's behalf?"

"Yes." The flow of tears resumed.

"Were you relieved when Haden and Serafina Wolf arrived and drove the coyote off?"

Bly sobbed and nodded. "Yes."

Legget didn't let up. "Did you think of going to thank the Wolfs?"

"Yes."

"Did you think that would be the right time to reclaim your child and curse whatever your family might have thought of him?"

More than anger returned to Bly's face; fury appeared.

"Yes!"

Lowering her voice, Legget asked, "But you didn't do that, did you?"

Bly shook her head. "No."

That might have been another place to stop, but there was one more point to make.

Legget said, "Mr. Fuentes has asserted, if I have it right, that a Native American mother has a claim to her child that none can match, but would you agree, Ms. Black Knife, that a Native American father has an equal claim?"

Emotional exhaustion shifted to bewilderment and Bly asked, "Billy?"

"Yes, Ms. Black Knife, Billy."

"I don't know where he is. I saw him only that one time."

"Technology is a marvel, Ms. Black Knife. We know the name of the rodeo you attended and the names of all the people who both worked and competed there."

Bly wasn't sure what Legget was getting at, but Fuentes knew.

The other side didn't have Billy yet, but if his heart were still beating they would find him.

Use him to stake a custody claim of his own. Maybe he'd do it because he'd love to have a son. Maybe he'd do it for money. But if the court ruled for Bly that wouldn't be the end of it.

Legget repeated, "Would Billy have a claim equal to your own?"

"I guess."

"Of course," Legget said, "were the two of you to marry, you'd have a stronger claim."

That idea was advanced for Maria and Cesar's benefit. Give the two of them a reason to drop the case. Bly's father might have died, but it was a good bet his attitudes lived on. Bringing up the idea at all carried a risk, but the Wolfs had given Legget their permission to use it.

"I don't even know Billy," Bly said.

Which was another point of character for the jury to consider.

Legget said, "I have no further questions."

The jury deliberated for less than an hour and returned a decision in favor of the Wolfs: Their adoption of John Tall Wolf would stand. Judge Marquez thanked the members of the jury for their service. He ordered Bly Black Knife to pay the Wolfs' legal fees.

No sooner had he finished speaking than Bly shocked everyone in the courtroom, except Haden and Serafina, by standing and telling the Wolfs, "To you, Coyote is just an animal, but we know he is much more. He will never rest until he takes the child you claim as yours."

Before the judge could rebuke Bly, Serafina rose and said, "We *do* know."

Knew so well, Bly turned and left the courtroom. The judge let well enough alone.

On the courthouse steps, though, Perico Fuentes had his own warning. He addressed it to Angeline Legget, but the Wolfs were with her, and they were Fuentes' primary audience.

Bly's lawyer said, "I'm going to appeal this court's decision. The Indian Child Welfare Act provides that in cases of concurrent jurisdiction, which is the case here, tribal courts shall be given preference. I'm sure we will win the appeal, and then we'll see how you do in tribal court."

Perico Fuentes had just played his ace.

So Angeline Legget played hers.

"Your client, Mr. Fuentes, claimed she didn't know why she didn't bring John into Santa Fe and leave him with someone who could guarantee his safety. But she knew perfectly well why she didn't do that. As a Native American infant, the local authorities would have had to return John to his tribe, and your client's father would have learned the truth his daughter didn't want him to know, not even at the cost of John's life. Your client placed her interests above all else."

"You can't prove my client knew the boy would be returned to the tribe," Fuentes said.

Legget smiled. "Mr. Fuentes, my cross-examination of your client was kid glove treatment. We go into tribal court, I'll take her apart. She thinks my clients should fear Coyote; she should fear me."

Fuentes grimaced but said, "We could still prevail."

"You might prevail, but the cost to the tribe's reputation would be ruinous. Think of it, a tribal court awarding custody to a woman who was willing to sacrifice her child to save her own reputation rather than let the child continue to live with the only parents he's ever known, the people who saved his life. There is no way to justify that, and I'll shred anyone who tries."

Before Fuentes could attempt a rebuttal, Legget added, "And don't forget Billy. We'll find him; you know we will."

Haden leaned in and whispered into Legget's ear.

Legget left Fuentes with one last thing to think about.

"My client makes an excellent point. If there's to be another trial, we will need to examine the character of the late Cesar Black Knife to learn just why his daughter and others feared him so. You really ought to reconsider the wisdom of appealing the current decision. Talk with Maria Black Knife and her son. See what they have to say."

Fuentes turned and walked away without another word.

***

Legal threats were all well and good, but Haden and Serafina weren't about to take any chances that they might lose their son. Not confiding in anyone, including their lawyer, they employed other methods to make sure John stayed with them. They began the night the trial ended.

Bly was visited by a terrible dream. Her son had been returned to her, but he hated her. Worse, everywhere she took him, Coyote lurked. Her own curse had come back to haunt her. One day soon, she knew, Coyote would take her child … and the Wolfs would be there to watch. They were always watching her now; there was no escape from them.

They would see when Coyote came for her son again.

Only this time they wouldn't intervene.

They would watch with pitiless eyes and see her fail to defend her child once more.

The first time the nightmare came, Bly awoke screaming. When it came again on the next two nights, Bly realized that Serafina had sent it to her, and she would not stop. The woman was a *bruja*. She might even have taught the child magic. Who knew what he might do to her?

Bly dropped her claim on John. She told her mother and brother if they pursued the case independently, she would testify for the Wolfs. Say they were the best ones to raise the child. Maria and Cesar had no desire to claim John; they now saw him as a threat to their plans to retain a place of prominence in the tribe.

Bly's change of heart worked in their favor, better than she might have guessed.

Now, they could say Bly had caused the tribe great embarrassment and expense.

She should leave the reservation, she was told.

She did, suffering exactly the fate her father would have visited on her.

CHAPTER 12

Santa Fe, New Mexico — June 5, 1997

John graduated from Saint John's College with a classical education and no real idea of what he wanted to do with his life. He'd worked part-time jobs for his parents and friends of the family since he was twelve, but none of the jobs had suggested any career path. The purpose of his labors had been to teach John the values of work and thrift. In that, they had been successful. He was not afraid to put in a full day and over the years he had saved ten thousand dollars.

Thrift was all the easier when Mom and Dad provided free room, board and education.

As a graduation gift, Haden and Serafina had matched John's savings dollar for dollar. The Wolfs' idea, as a family, was that John would use his money to travel the world for a year. Discover who he was. Find out what his vocational interests might be.

John's plan was to start the journey in Mexico, the ancestral land of his mother's family. From there he would go to England, Germany and Denmark, the countries from which his father's family came. After that, he would go where the wind and whim carried him.

Having the beginning of his itinerary plotted, he headed that bright June morning to a travel agency to see what the experts might suggest as places around the world a young man ought not to miss. He never got that far. His car was pulled over by an unmarked sedan with flashing lights and a siren.

In other places, John might have been alarmed by such a turn of events. His copper complexion and the sunglasses he wore might have cast him as a figure of suspicion to some white cops in the southern United States. In Santa Fe, though, he was just another local. So what was the reason for —

John was taken by surprise when a woman with fashion model looks and clothes got out of the sedan. He'd never seen any cop who looked like her. In fact, her copper complexion looked a lot like his. Native American. Not quite Apache, Navajo or Hopi; she must have been from a more distant tribe. She was a bit older than him, too. Maybe thirty to his twenty-two.

John lowered his window as she came to stand beside his car.

"I do something wrong, Officer?" he asked.

She flashed a brilliant white smile at him, and showed her ID.

Marlene Flower Moon. Bureau of Indian Affairs. The woman was a fed.

"So this isn't a traffic stop?" John asked.

Ms. Flower Moon told him, "My hope is it's the start of a job interview."

"Where'd you get the cop car?" John asked.

"I borrowed it from the tribal police."

Remembering the words of warning his parents had imparted to him since he was a boy, John asked, "You're not Coyote, are you?"

Marlene said, "Let's talk and you can decide for yourself."

CHAPTER 13

Austin, Texas — July 11, the present

Marlene Flower Moon assured Detective Darton Blake that any information she or John turned up that was relevant to the murder of Randy Bear Heart would be relayed to the Austin Police Department.

Darton, having gotten to his feet, looked her in the eye, smiled and said, "Yes, ma'am."

Not that he believed her for a minute. He'd worked with the feds before. John T. might be cut from a different cloth, but this lady was pure Washington. He was glad he didn't have to answer to her.

"And you'll keep us informed of anything you learn?" Marlene said.

"Absolutely, ma'am. I'll be in touch with Special Agent Tall Wolf."

Marlene gave the local cop a smile as phony as the one he'd given her.

Then she took John to lunch.

Marlene knew a place that had been opened by a former bootlegger named Threadgill. John took a look around. Glanced at the menu. Ordered the special of the day, chicken enchiladas with two veggies. He asked for an ice tea to go with his meal.

Marlene echoed his order.

After the waitress left, he asked Marlene, "This place start out as a gas station?"

"It did," she said. "Janis Joplin used to sing here."

John nodded. His parents had one of Joplin's albums, but she'd died before John had been born. Marlene couldn't have been much more than an elementary school student back then.

"You like retro rock?" John asked.

"I like to see how people deal with their demons," she said.

John thought that was creepy, didn't ask to hear more.

"You have something job related to tell me?" he asked.

"I've been talking to people in South Dakota," Marlene said. "I spoke with some of Randy Bear Heart's old girlfriends, them and the secretary of the Mercy Ridge board of directors."

"You do all this by phone?" he asked.

"In person," she said.

John was surprised. It took a lot to get Marlene out of D.C.

She had to keep an eye on the store. Tend to her political interests.

"Don't look at me like that," she said. "I traveled to New Mexico to recruit you."

When they'd both been younger and Marlene had only started to climb her career ladder.

"Yes, you did," he said.

"You still think I'm a Chickahominy at heart."

The tribe was indigenous to Northern Virginia, a tomahawk throw from Washington.

John said, "What you've told me is you're a lineal descendant of Powhattan. But then the Algonquin are from that part of the country, too. Or so I'm informed."

Before joining the BIA, John knew little of the history of native peoples in North America. They hadn't figured in his scholastic education and given his history he had eschewed any personal interest. He'd learned more since signing on with Marlene. Did the assigned reading.

"Don't you think it would be interesting to have a Native American president?" she asked.

John smiled. "You are Coyote."

"Maybe," she replied.

John's relationship with Marlene over the years had traveled a narrow path from being professional to being insubordinate. From the start, Marlene had shown an interest in him that went beyond being a mentor to a protégé. He probably would have made some bad choices with her if Mom and Dad hadn't warned him about the Trickster.

John said, "A Native American president would be poetic, historic and ironic."

"And I'm icky enough to be all that?"

"No doubt."

"Or would I have to beat my drum and do the Ghost Dance?"

There was a belief among many Native Americans that the Ghost Dance would bring a great flood that would wash away all the white people and the Indians who hadn't traveled the Red Road, the path of native righteousness. In short, guys like John. But for the faithful the world after the flood would be just like the good old days. No white men and lots of buffalo.

"I'm not sure you've followed the Red Road any better than I have," John said.

"Maybe an exception or two can be made."

John laughed. "You certainly have the right attitude for politics."

Marlene smiled, a facial expression that John always thought of as a restrained snarl, something that might change in a flash to a snap of teeth and jaws. Coyote. But a wolf did not fear lesser canines. It devoured them.

In a fair fight, anyway.

Where trickery was involved, a guy had to be careful.

Marlene told him, "I wanted to talk with Annie Forger while I was in South Dakota."

"Wanted?" John asked.

"She was nowhere to be found. Her house in Rapid City is empty. The utilities have been turned off."

John frowned. "You asked around, the white cops as well as

the red?"

Marlene nodded. "Nobody knows anything."

"Or nobody's talking."

"See what you can find out," Marlene told John.

There were times when Marlene truly wanted him to do his job, John knew, and there were other times when she wanted him to *look* like he was conducting an investigation. That had disconcerted him early in his career. If she didn't want him to do things the right way, why had she ...

He came to realize she'd hired him to produce the results that were politically advantageous to her. If not, there was no reason to hire a guy who had no more cultural awareness of Native Americans than your average white man. In other words, precious little. But he did have one important advantage.

He looked the part. Marlene's interface with the white world had a red face. His biological heritage let him pass as a native, and he'd used that to his advantage. His physical appearance was the best disguise an undercover cop could ask for. Marlene's mistake, though, was assuming John thought like a typical white man.

Yes, his father, Haden Wolf, had white skin, had gone to medical school and not only wore a white collar but also a white coat. Dad's appearance, however, was even more deceiving than John's. Haden Wolf had a family background of folk magicians, herbalists and diviners. His thought processes were as fluid as a river during a spring flood.

Mom was Dad's soulmate. Her family, the Padillas, was a mix of *indios* and *conquistadores*, *curanderos* and *brujas*. The Padillas and their forebears had been casting spells for both good and ill since pre-Colombian times. Like her husband, Serafina had added contemporary scientific study to her wealth of knowledge.

Neither parent saw any reason why their son shouldn't be raised in both communities: folk wisdom and lab testing.

Outwitting Marlene Flower Moon and doing his job the way he saw fit was John's greatest professional joy. He might or might not return to South Dakota to see what had become of Annie Forger. But right now Ms. Forger's whereabouts were a side issue, a distraction.

John intended to stay in Austin and find out how Randy Bear Heart had met his end.

John dropped Marlene off at Austin-Bergstrom International Airport for her flight back to Washington. He told her he'd be reporting in as soon as he found out anything important. If she wanted to interpret that to mean he would be complying with her wish to have him go back to South Dakota, so be it.

She could commiserate with SAC Gilbert Melvin on what a prick John was.

CHAPTER 14

Austin, Texas — July 12, the present

Detective Darton Blake picked John up at The Driskill Hotel in downtown Austin. He'd checked out of his room at the La Quinta near the airport. He assumed that Marlene had suborned someone at his former lodgings to let her know if he continued to stay there. The Driskill was a four-star hotel; its rates were well above John's per diem for putting a roof over his head. As long as he made up the difference out of his pocket, though, there would be no problem. He caught a break when the Driskill's manager, a patriotic Texas lady, saw his credentials and offered to comp his room.

John couldn't let her do that, but he was agreeable to having her let the federal government pay its usual toll.

"Nice digs," Darton said as John got into his car.

"Very nice."

"This the kind of place the BIA puts up all its people?"

John didn't want his new partner to get irate over the misuse of his tax dollars so he gave Darton the backstory. The detective smiled.

"That's cool, but you're not going to catch grief from Ms. Flower Moon?"

"Marlene and I play push and pull all the time," he said.

Darton gave him a look.

"In terms of our professional relationship," John elaborated.

"Good to know," the detective said. He pulled into an opening in traffic. "I might have a lead on Randy Bear Heart."

"Tell me," John said.

"Well, it's been my experience that most fugitives outsmart themselves."

John nodded. He had the same understanding of cons on the run.

"Sometimes they miss a little detail; sometimes they screw up so bad you wonder if they manage to put their boots on the right feet."

"I can go along with a small slip-up," John said, "but Randy Bear Heart was supposed to be one smart Native American."

"Yeah, and how many smart guys have you seen do dumb things?"

"Ego can get in the way," John allowed.

"Okay, then. Looking for something really dumb, I wanted to see if a pretty boy like Randy came to town and wanted to make a living smiling for the camera. Like being a model or something."

Annie Forger had said Randy was crazy, John thought.

Still, he said, "Don't tell me he was that stuck on himself."

"No, he was too smart for that, but he had the bad luck of fathering a son who was his spitting image. A girl at one of the talent agencies in town that I sent Randy's picture to recognized him. Only she thought the picture was his kid, Jackson."

John asked, "Jackson did something in the public eye?"

Darton stopped for a red light and nodded.

"Acting?" John asked, thinking of Randy's fascination with Warren Beatty.

"We get some movies shot around here, but where we're really big is music."

"Jackson was in a band?"

Darton smiled and stepped on the gas as the light turned green.

"He was the front man. Singer, songwriter and co-lead guitarist."

"Damn," John said. "How could he be more obvious?"

"I'll tell you how. He named his band after a certain lawman who died in South Dakota."

"Red Hawk?"

"You got it. That's actually a pretty cool name for a country-rock band."

John shook his head. He wondered if the ghost of the murdered cop had inspired the choice of the band's name ... and then had a good laugh about what happened next. There were times when John's rational view of life disappeared like a puff of smoke in a high wind. Spirits and magic ruled the world.

He was glad Marlene Flower Moon had never been around when he felt that shift in perception. He feared he might look up and see she really was Coyote. As it was, he could almost hear her howling now.

"Has she gone?" a man's voice asked.

John remembered going into police headquarters and sitting down next to Darton's desk in the homicide unit. He didn't, however, recall when SAC Melvin had entered the picture. He pulled his head out of the clouds.

"Who?" John asked.

"Pocahontas, the killer Indian queen," the FBI man said.

"Yeah, she's gone," Darton said.

Maybe, John thought.

He asked Melvin, "She ruffles the Bureau's feathers?"

"Feathers? Yeah, that's a good one. Fact is, Marlene scares most of official Washington."

"You think she'll go on the warpath?" John asked.

"What I think is, a lot of people will be working for her someday — those of us who can't collect our pensions first."

Maybe Marlene will become president, John thought.

"She scares you that much?" Darton asked.

"How'd you like to work for her?" Melvin replied.

Darton saw his point.

"Either of you gentlemen come up with anything I should know?" Melvin asked. "You know, something I might have the resources to deal with that you don't."

Darton looked at John, silently asking if he should share his news about Jackson.

John told Melvin, "Annie Forger, the woman I interviewed in Rapid City, South Dakota, the former girlfriend of Randy Bear Heart: She suddenly left home. Her house is vacant and the utilities have been turned off. No one knows where she is."

"This was right after you talked to her?" Melvin asked.

"Don't know if it was *right* after. I learned of it last night. Pocahontas told me."

Melvin grunted.

John told him, "I believe your organization has offices in all fifty states. Finding Ms. Forger might be just the thing for you."

Melvin thought about that and said, "Unless Annie Forger is holed up at Mercy Ridge or some other Indian trust land. Then it's your job, Mr. BIA man."

John stood up and told Melvin, "I don't do reservations."

He left the two white guys looking at each other while he went to the can.

When John got back from the men's room, Melvin had left.

"You tell him anything about Jackson and Red Hawk?" John asked.

Darton shook his head. "The way I see it, this is your case. I'll just follow your play."

"Thanks." John took a seat. "There's more to the story of Ms. Forger. Her husband died and she received a three-million-dollar life insurance benefit. So, if she wants, I bet she can make a good, long run."

"What'd her husband do?" Darton asked.

"Played pro hockey in Vancouver, BC. His name was Vern Forger. He died in a car crash in L.A with two teammates, one of whom was supposed to be the designated driver, but toked up anyway."

John let Darton chew on that for a minute.

Then John said, "I can see how having Marlene looking for you might incline a person to run. Might even lead other people to grab Annie before Marlene could get to her. Marlene said I should look into Annie's vanishing act, but I'm going to work Austin with you for a while, if you have no objection."

"None whatsoever," Darton said.

"Good. Let's go see if there are any Red Hawk fans in town."

CHAPTER 15

Santa Fe, New Mexico — June 5, 1997

" I won't work on a reservation," John told Marlene Flower Moon first thing.

His job interview had taken place at The Pink Adobe. It was lunchtime, but he didn't want to make even an implied commitment by ordering a meal. He ordered the Chocolate Denise, a mousse with fresh whipped cream, the house specialty.

Marlene had a salad. John saw how she could keep her figure eating light like that, but he'd bet the lady liked her protein, too. Something cooked blood rare.

John had kept his voice down when he made his declaration. Some of the diners were Native American. He wasn't looking to put any noses out of joint; he was just making a point.

Marlene spoke quietly, too, but her tone was sharp.

"What's the problem, Mr. Tall Wolf? Third world poverty right here in the USA disturb you?"

"You didn't just find me on the street, Ms. Flower Moon. You checked me out, didn't you?"

She nodded, keeping her face impassive.

"Then you know my story. You know Bly Black Knife tried to take me away from my parents and bring me back to the rez."

She surprised John by saying, "I first heard of you by visiting the rez."

"What?"

"I spoke with your grandmother."

John had heard of Maria Black Knife but he'd never met her.

Then Marlene pushed things a step further.

"If you're interested, your birth mother died last year."

It was a rare day when John thought of the woman at all … but he was curious.

Not that he came out and asked for details. Marlene told him anyway.

After filling him in on some other points of interest.

"The tribal lawyer, a Mr. Fuentes, if I remember right, wanted to appeal the decision that awarded you to the Wolfs. But Bly said if he appealed she would testify on behalf of your adoptive parents."

That was another jolt, and Ms. Flower Moon was watching to see how he responded.

"Why would she do that?" John asked in a flat voice.

"Depends on who's asking. The outside world would hear that she didn't want to go through the torment of another trial. I was told privately by a shaman that Serafina Wolf y Padilla sent a dream to Bly that terrified her so badly she couldn't go through with the appeal."

John did his best to keep a smile of pride off his face.

"So she got scared."

"*Terrified.* That was the exact word I was given."

John got the feeling Marlene wanted him to tell her about a woman with such power.

He declined to share any information about his mother.

Marlene continued her story. "Shortly after that, having fallen out of favor with her family, Bly left the reservation. She went to Flagstaff and found work as a waitress. The son of the restaurant's owner fell in love with her and they married. They had a good life, until a gas leak in their house asphyxiated both of them. The fire department found them in bed with their arms around each other. Tragic but peaceful."

John thought about that. Wondered if someone had arranged the leak.

Did Coyote know HVAC?

John said, "So you just happened to be on the rez and heard all this?"

"Part of my job is to scout young Native American people with talent."

"And Bly's mother knew all about me?"

Marlene said, "You and your grandmother live near each other. You go about your life openly."

"I didn't know anyone was spying on me."

Marlene smiled. "Well, you know how stealthy Indians can be."

John knew Marlene was mocking him. He ignored it. "What's Maria's interest in me?"

"She wants to make sure you don't upset her plans."

"What plans?" he asked.

"Bly's brother, Cesar, was supposed to be the coming power among his people, but he died in an accident, too. His Jeep went off a mountain road."

Latin was one of the languages John had studied at St. John's College. Among the phrases he'd learned was *cui bono?* Who benefits? Lawyers liked to use it.

"Did that work out for anybody," he asked, "Bly and Cesar dying."

"Well, in Cesar's place, his son Arnoldo seems to be doing well. Your grandmother is grooming him for a long run in a position of power. She wants to make sure you never intend to return to the reservation and become a rival to your cousin. What she didn't say, but what she really wants, is for you to return and Arnoldo to vanquish you."

John laughed. "Did she ask to hear from you after we had this little talk?"

"She did."

"Okay, here's what you tell Granny: Don't worry about a thing. I'm never coming back."

The main purpose of the BIA was to facilitate government-to-government relations between the United States and 565 federally recognized tribes with a combined population of just under two million American Indians and Alaska natives. The people of those tribes, in recent years, had placed an increasing emphasis on self-governance, but they still looked to the BIA for assistance with such things as social services and natural resource management of trust lands.

In some of the most economically disadvantaged places, economic development programs were provided.

The BIA also helped with law and order: cops, jails and tribal courts.

John's official role, as a federal agent, was to act as a liaison between Native American cops and those in the larger society. When major crimes against persons were committed by one side against the other, it was his responsibility to see that resolution, if not justice, was achieved without wholesale bloodshed.

Given his upbringing and his insistence, John was an outside man.

Outside the rez.

Other cops worked as inside men.

That hadn't been the usual way of things, but Marlene had taken the lemon John had handed her and made lemonade.

Had John been limited to his official duties, he would have turned down Marlene's job offer. But he had another responsibility, not listed in his job description, that intrigued him. While he worked for the BIA, he was an unacknowledged shadow agent for the EPA.

Native Americans believed fervently that they were the stewards of the earth. They wanted to be sure that when Great Spirit restored the land and the buffalo to them the planet would be a healthy place.

"Restored?" John had asked Marlene.

"Our ancestors," she said, "yours and mine, have been in this land for at least twelve thousand years and maybe as long as twenty thousand years. You really think the white man will last that long?"

John knew there were some Native Americans who believed their ancestors had *always* lived in North America. That immigration from Asia stuff? Forget it. That story about Africa being the cradle of humanity? No way.

At the time, John simply shook his head and told Marlene, "In case you haven't noticed, there are plenty of black, brown and yellow people in the country these days. Are all of them transients, too?"

"If they're white inside."

"Like me," he said.

"Like you think you are."

John's mother had warned him about women who might try to save him from himself.

He said, "If I help prevent environmental damage, that'll be good for *everyone,* not just one group of people."

"If that's how you want to see it," Marlene said, showing him her unsettling smile.

John refused to either be seduced or to lose his temper, but he took the job.

After he negotiated another ten grand in starting pay — and the freedom to pursue his cases as he saw fit.

Marlene had asked with a laugh, "You want a license to take scalps, too?"

"That'd be good," John said.

The BIA sent John to the Federal Law Enforcement Training Center in Glynco, Georgia where none of the male feds had hair long enough to be worth taking.

All the trainees took the same curriculum: interviewing, surveillance, criminal case management, legal training, physical conditioning and self-defense techniques, tactical training, firearms proficiency, vehicle handling skills and physical evidence collection.

After becoming proficient in those skills, John was sent back to New Mexico for more training: back country tactics and tracking.

The course lasted five days. John paid attention and learned all he could — all the while thinking Marlene was cosseted in Washington laughing at him, thinking she'd made an Indian of him after all.

What she didn't know — at least he thought she didn't — was that John had taken more wilderness trips with his parents than he could remember. He'd learned things that neither the BIA or anyone else in the federal government had ever dreamed of.

Except for maybe a few of the wizards at DARPA.

The Defense Advance Research Projects Agency.

The Pentagon's version of Hogwarts.

Joseph Flynn

CHAPTER 16

Austin, Texas — July 12, the present

Detective Darton Blake had engaged in serious understatement when he'd said Austin was really big in music.

The town called itself The Live Music Capital of the World. Had even trademarked the name. There were two hundred live music stages in town. You wanted rock, blues, jazz or country, there were clubs and venues for you. You were feeling in a classical mood, the city had its own symphony orchestra. The center of the music scene was Sixth Street, but adjacent neighborhoods were not to be overlooked.

John and Darton lost count of all the clubs they'd visited looking for Jackson White, as he'd styled himself as a musician. Almost everyone they talked to either remembered Jackson or had heard of him, but no one could recall seeing him for years. That was a real shame, too, many people said, because the guy was talented. Had the whole package musically: could write, play and sing.

Of the people they'd talked to, most of them asked John and Darton to give them a call if they found out what Jackson was up to these days. Four club managers said they'd be happy to book him, if he was still in the game.

Hours into their search, they caught a break by stopping into a diner on Fourth Street for lunch and John whimsically asking their waitress if she knew where Jackson White was hanging out these days.

She asked the obvious question, "He a musician?"

"*Virtuoso*," Darton said.

The waitress gave him a squint. "That Spanish?"

John said, "Italian. Means he's really good."

She smiled and nodded. "Have to remember that, virtuoso. Anyway, if the fella was all that good, the guy you want to ask is Larry Taggart. Used to cover the music beat for the *American Statesman* for about a hundred years. Now, he's got his own Internet site."

"How do we find him?" Darton asked.

The waitress cocked her head. "His office is that last booth next to the kitchen. Larry likes his food hot."

John, who'd agreed to buy lunch for Darton, tipped the waitress one hundred percent of their check, including the tax.

Larry Taggart was willing to have the lawmen sit down with him, and once he heard they weren't interested in anything to do with the personal use of marijuana he agreed to listen to their story.

"Jackson White?" Taggart said. "That young man was something special, had himself a real generous muse and a loving relationship with his six string, could make that guitar shout and whisper, cry and laugh." The music writer looked at John. "Never figured he'd have done anything to bring federal attention to himself."

John said, "He didn't. His father was a bad guy. We're looking for Jackson to help us clear up a few things."

Darton nodded in agreement.

Weighing the character of the two cops facing him, Taggart said, "Hope I don't regret telling you fellas this, but if there's anyone who might help you it's Coy Wilson."

"And Coy Wilson is?" John asked.

"She was Jackson's special lady. Played co-lead guitar, rhythm guitar and keyboard in Red Hawk. Sang harmony and wrote some of their songs with Jackson. Does studio work now is what I hear."

"She live in town?" Darton asked.

Taggart took an iPad out of a leather courier's bag on the seat next to him. He tapped its screen a few times and slid the tablet over to John and Darton's side of the table.

"There you go," he said. "Still listed in the phone directory."

Darton copied the information.

John bought Taggart's lunch, too.

Back in Darton's car, the detective told John, "That was a pretty good play, asking that waitress about Jackson White."

"I get lucky sometimes," John said.

"My favorite kind of person to work with," Darton said.

Coy Wilson lived on a quiet block of single-family homes within walking distance of the University of Texas campus. No one answered the doorbell after three increasingly lengthy rings, but a peek through a front window showed the house still looked occupied and furnished by someone with financial means and an artful eye.

Darton took out a business card and wrote a please-call-me note on it.

He was about to drop it into Ms. Wilson's mailbox when a next door neighbor stepped halfway out of his house and asked, "Something I can help you gentlemen with?"

The man was at least in his sixties, judging by the gray in his hair, but he still looked fit and was smart enough to be able to duck back inside if he didn't like their answer.

Darton took out his badge. "I'm Detective Blake with the Austin PD, and this gentleman is a federal officer. We'd like to speak with Ms. Wilson. Is there anything you might do to help us?"

"My name's Lloyd Rucker, and I can tell you Coy's working in L.A., but she's supposed to be home tomorrow — if the recording session doesn't run long."

John asked, "Have you ever seen a man called Jackson White at Ms. Wilson's home?"

"Sure, Jackson lived there with Coy, but not for quite some time."

"You knew him?" Darton asked.

"In a neighborly way. He's a talented young man. Handsome. Great personality. He and Coy would bring beer and barbecue over to my house. I'd keep an eye out for their place when they were on the road."

Darton asked, "He and Ms. Wilson ever rehearse in her house?"

John added, "If they did, was the music ever too loud for you?"

Rucker laughed. "What they did was write their songs in that house, and my only complaint about the volume was I had to ask them to turn it up, my hearing not being what it used to be."

"They were that good?" John asked.

"Yes, they were. Coy still is, I imagine, but I don't hear her play or sing at home anymore. Must do all her music in the studio these days. A real shame from my point of view."

"She and Jackson break up?" Darton asked.

Rucker sighed. "I tried as gently as I could to ask about that one time. Coy just gave me a sad smile and I didn't ask again. Anything else I can do for you?"

Darton gave Rucker the business card he'd inscribed for Coy.

"If Ms. Wilson doesn't come home tomorrow, I'd appreciate a call."

"You bet." Lloyd Rucker went back inside his home.

John and Darton looked at each other.

"Love and heartbreak?" Darton asked.

John shrugged. "Life imitating art, maybe."

CHAPTER 17

Treaty Oak Park, Austin, Texas — July 12, the present

Unable to find Jackson White or talk to Coy Wilson, John and Darton stopped by the Whole Foods Market on the corner of Lamar and Sixth and got something healthy to drink. Darton had a Cherry Vanilla Cream All Natural Soda; John went with a Republic of Tea Cranberry Blood Orange tea. They walked to nearby Treaty Oak Park.

The ground on which the park was set once served as a sacred meeting place for the Comanche and Tonkawa tribes. The Treaty Oak was estimated to be five hundred years old. Darton did not do the tourist guide bit and inform John of the park's history. Nor did John ask if Darton had chosen the setting for any reason other than a park bench in the shade of a tree beat sitting in a hot car as a place to work.

Each of them used his laptop to check the law enforcement databases to which he had access. Entering the names Lily White Bird and Lily Red Hawk, John came up with no returns. Darton didn't find anything under those names either. But he did find a Lily White.

He told John, "I figured if Jackson used the name White, maybe he got it from mama."

"Good thinking. What'd she commit a misdemeanor or a felony?"

"Neither," Darton said. "She's on record for committing good deeds not bad ones. Ms. White made annual contributions to the

Austin Fallen Officers' Fund. Our widows and orphans charity."

John authored a thin smile. "Either the woman has a guilty conscience or she likes her irony."

"You think she regrets the death of Daniel Red Hawk?" Darton asked.

"That or she's trying to atone, set herself up for a better spot in the next world."

Darton nodded. "Some do get religion, if they're able to tell right from wrong."

"Is Ms. White current in trying to make amends?"

"No, last donation was four years ago."

John thought about that. Frowned.

Seeing his expression, Darton asked, "What?"

"I'm wondering if maybe that was about the time Jackson stopped playing Austin."

Darton bobbed his head. "Just because we haven't said it doesn't mean we both haven't thought it: Jackson White is dead."

"That'd give his mother another regret to occupy her mind."

"Might give us another possibility for the body in the lake bed," Darton said.

"That, too," John agreed.

Darton told him, "You know, I'm pretty good about attending the annual Fallen Officers fundraiser. I don't recall seeing a Native American lady among the honored guests. Not surprising if she wanted to preserve her anonymity. She just sends in a check with the name Lily White on it, we might think she was a Daughter of the Confederacy. Show up in person, she'd change all that."

John got to his feet, "Let's see if we can find Ms. White. Pay her a visit."

Darton stood and said, "I already have a lead on that. Her donation checks were drawn on a business account."

"What's the name of the business?"

Darton said, "It's a place called Go Native."

Go Native was a boutique in Austin's SoCo neighborhood. It

featured contemporary artists who fashioned Native American themed art, furnishings and accessories. Its location in the hip South of Congress location couldn't have been better. But the lights in the shop were dimmed, the door was locked and a sign said closed for inventory.

No one was present in the showroom, but there was a light on in a back room.

Darton called Austin Telephone, identified himself, gave his badge number and asked if Go Native had an unlisted business number. He wanted the line the store used to make outgoing calls, not the one that would be answered by voice mail, telling him what he already knew: the store was closed. He got the number he wanted.

A second call and a minute later, a good-looking fiftyish blonde stepped out of the back room and crossed to the front door. She made sure she got a long look at both John and Darton's badges, before she let them inside. She relocked the door behind them.

She was more interested in John than Darton.

"You're with the BIA?"

"Yes, ma'am."

"I'll turn up the lights in the shop. You can check every item I have. As far as I know, there's nothing in the store I'm not supposed to have."

Darton was confused. "What kind of items are you not supposed to have?"

John told his new friend. "I believe the lady is referring to ceremonial objects white people are not meant to see much less buy and sell."

The woman nodded, then realized she'd forgotten her manners.

"I'm sorry. I haven't introduced myself. I'm Barbara Larson. I own Go Native."

She shook hands with both men.

John told her, "We have no question about the goods in your store, Ms. Larson. Don't worry about that."

"Then what would the BIA want with … Is this something to

do with Lily?"

"You know Lily White Bird, Ms. Larson?" Darton asked.

"Of course, I do." She paused to look at a couple peering at the goods in the shop's display window. "Would you mind if we talk in back? I really can't open to the public right now."

She led John and Darton to an office in the back, got them seated and seemed relieved that they didn't want anything to drink.

Sitting behind her desk, Barbara said, "Of course, I know Lily. I worked for her; I bought the store from her. When she decided to sell, two years after I started here, I talked to my husband, Bob, and we bought the place. I run it." She took a moment to think and look at Darton. "You said Lily White Bird, but this was the only place she used her full name. Everywhere else she was just Lily White."

John said, "Did Ms. White say why she wanted to sell the business?"

"She said she wanted to move to the San Diego area and open a new shop there. We agreed we could both use the name Go Native. We joked that maybe we could go national, build a whole chain of ..." Barbara Larson's face took a sudden fall. "Please don't tell me something bad has happened to Lily."

"We don't know of anything like that," John said. "We're looking for her regarding another matter. Have you heard from her since you bought the store?"

Barbara shook her head and the corners of her mouth turned down.

John had failed to reassure her.

That or some other unhappy thought had entered her mind.

"Something occur to you just now, Ms. Larson?" Darton asked.

"Yes, it did. Lily never said so but I got the feeling she was going to California to get away from her husband."

"Just your opinion?" John said.

Barbara Larson took a deep breath and let it go slowly.

"I might be all wrong about this. It was one of those situations where there are holes in the conversations you have with someone you're coming to know. Things you can feel the other person isn't telling you. With Lily, it was her husband. I recognized what she wasn't saying because that was how I was with my first husband."

Darton said, "If you don't mind us asking, Ms. Larson —"

"I don't talk about Roy because, to put it in plain Texan, he was a cheatin' sumbitch. The kind that won't ever change."

John said, "You don't think you're wrong, do you, Ms. Larson, about Lily's husband being her problem?"

Barbara looked John in the eye.

"No, I don't."

CHAPTER 18

Austin, Texas — July 13, the present

Coy Wilson was operating on three hours of sleep when the limo pulled up in front of her house. The driver offered to carry her suitcase and guitar case to the door. Coy thanked him, tipped him and said that wouldn't be necessary. She had heard stories of limo drivers in L.A. toting luggage to a woman's door, pushing in after her and raping her. California was ahead of the curve with most things, including innovative predators, but Coy didn't want to take any chances that the bad guys in Austin weren't quick learners.

She'd no sooner stepped out of the limo than she saw she needn't have worried. Two big men stepped up to her holding their badges. Cops. Most likely. There had been cases of psychos impersonating cops in L.A., too. But when she saw one of the men in front of her was from the Bureau of Indian Affairs her knees started to buckle.

A cop caught her under each arm. The Indian guy in the sunglasses — she could see he looked Native American now — caught her guitar case, too, before it hit the ground.

The limo driver popped out of the car, wanting to make sure Coy was all right.

Darton turned his badge in the driver's direction. "Austin PD. The young lady is perfectly safe. Thank you for your concern."

The driver read between the lines. He got in his car and left.

But not without making a call, Darton saw. No doubt to the

police to check on the story he'd been given. Good man.

Coy looked at John. "Is this about Jackson? Is he dead?"

Coy invited the two cops into her home, but she didn't offer them food or drink. She was surfing a wave of fear and adrenaline, but fatigue still tugged at her eyelids. If the cops had something bad to tell her, she'd just give in and black out.

She didn't want to repeat her question, so she just looked at the Native American cop.

John told her, "We're hoping to find Jackson White, Ms. Wilson. We don't know whether he's alive or not."

"You think I know?" Coy asked. "After what I just asked you?"

Darton told her. "Some people try to mislead the police, Ms. Wilson."

She'd heard him tell the limo driver he was a city cop. "I'm not one of them. Lying to you would be stupid." She turned to look at John. "But lying to you would be a crime, right? You're a fed."

"I am, and it is a crime to lie to a federal officer. People still do, though. I'll take you at your word that you're not one of them."

She gave him a look and said, "Because musicians are so trustworthy?"

"Because I don't think you'd drop your guitar on purpose," John said.

Tears formed in Coy's eyes. "No, I wouldn't. Jesus, let's get some coffee. I hope you can stomach the instant stuff."

"Jackson's father is dead?" Coy asked, stirring a second spoon of sugar into her coffee.

Neither John nor Darton had accepted her offer of a cup.

Nor had they told her that maybe it was Jackson's body that had been found.

What Darton said was, "Randy Bear Heart had been wanted by the FBI for bank robbery. He'd been flying under the radar for a long time, but my son found remains in the Lake Travis mud that appear to be his."

"Your son?" Coy asked.

"Strange old world, isn't it?" Darton said.

Coy turned to John, "And you got involved because Randy was Native American?"

John said, "One of the three cops he killed was on the Mercy Ridge Reservation."

He didn't say the cop's name was Red Hawk. Didn't want her to break down.

"Oh, God. Did Jackson know all this stuff?"

"We don't know," John said. "He was very young at the time."

Darton told Coy, "A forensic anthropologist came up with a sketch of the victim's face based on the contours of the skull." He handed a copy to Coy.

Anticipating a reaction, Darton reached for the coffee cup Coy held; John moved close to make sure she didn't slip off her chair, but it was the woman's jaw that dropped and nothing else.

"My God," she sobbed. "It *is* Jackson."

Darton took the cup from her, just in case.

John handed her a copy of the photo of Randy Bear Heart and Lily White Bird in their Bonnie and Clyde attire. Coy's sorrow turned to anger in a flash.

"Who the hell's the bimbo with Jackson?" she demanded. "And what's with the cos—" The tirade stopped in mid-word as Coy realized what she was looking at. "That's Lily, Jackson's mom, under that blonde wig. Looking a lot younger than when I knew her. Is the guy with her Jackson's dad?"

John nodded.

"I never met him. Damn, they couldn't look more alike."

John and Darton exchanged a glance. They had yet to find a photo of Randy Bear Heart as an adult. They watched as Coy reexamined the anthropologist's sketch and compared it to the photo of Randy Bear Heart.

She looked up at Darton.

"That body your son found could be either of them."

"Can you guess why Jackson left town, Ms. Wilson?" John

asked.

"I don't have to guess, I know. Partly anyway. Jackson and I were in bed when he got a call from Lily. I know because I answered the phone. All she said to me was could she talk to her son, but it sounded like she was trying hard not to cry. Jackson listened a minute and told her he'd be right over. When he got off the phone he had a look on his face like nothing I'd ever seen before. He just told me he had to go.

"I asked when he'd be coming back. He said as soon as he could, but he never did. All I could think was he and his mother had gotten into some terrible trouble and had to run."

"You never went to the police?" Darton asked.

Coy looked at him. "And say what? I didn't know what happened. Shit, there are times when I'm down on myself that I think it was all a real mean joke the two of them played on me."

John asked in a soft voice, "If it were a joke, wouldn't Jackson have continued his musical career?"

The epiphany hammered Coy. "Of course, he would have."

She looked back at the sketch of the dead man and began to cry.

Before Coy could sink too deeply into despair, John asked, "The look on Jackson's face, the one you'd never seen before, would it fit with a man thinking of killing someone?"

Coy's sorrow was derailed by the new surprise. "That was exactly what it looked like."

Before they left, Darton went to get Coy's neighbor, Lloyd Rucker, to come sit with her.

SAC Gilbert Melvin sat in his borrowed Austin office and reviewed the latest information to come from the medical specialists who'd examined the skeletal remains taken from Lake Travis. Somebody named Antoinette Portis, M.D. had figured out the age at death of the murder victim. There was an explanation of the reasoning that led to her conclusion, laid out in words a layman could understand.

Science these days was amazing stuff, Melvin thought.

Things might get to the point where the people in the lab coats and the guys in the SWAT squads were the only cops anybody needed.

Right now, though, he had an edge on John Tall Wolf.

Oh, he'd make the information available, upon request.

Maybe he'd send it *postal* mail to Tall Wolf.

Meanwhile, he left a voicemail at Darton Blake's number telling his counterparts he'd been in touch with Marlene Flower Moon. Let them think he was passing the good stuff along promptly.

"Ms. Flower Moon told me the people at Mercy Ridge informed her that none of their sacred relics is missing. Maybe that's all she'd tell … someone from another agency." Melvin wasn't about to say all she'd tell a white guy on a voice recording. "Perhaps Special Agent Tall Wolf should contact her directly and see if she has more details for him."

Melvin ended the call just as another thought occurred to him.

What if Bear Heart *had* stolen something special, and the Indians had caught up with him and gotten their goods back?

Melvin was going to keep that thought to himself.

If it turned out to be true, it was going to be a political hot potato.

That he'd toss to Tall Wolf.

CHAPTER 19

The Road to Austin, Texas — August, 1986

Lily White Bird came to regret killing her husband, Daniel Red Hawk, but not immediately. When she'd had her last argument with Randy, a month before she'd married Red Hawk, Lily had summed up her feelings by telling Randy, "I don't want to see you again until you're old and ugly."

After Randy had sent the unsigned note apologizing to her, he'd come to her house and greeted her by asking, "Old and ugly enough for you yet?"

Randy still looked so good he made her heart race.

Before she could have any second thoughts, he leaned in close and kissed her.

To feel his lips again was all it took. She pulled him inside the house, took a look to make sure no one had been watching and closed the door. Drew the threadbare curtains, too.

In bed, afterward, he admitted to her, "I haven't changed, but I've slowed down some."

Lily laughed.

"What?" Randy asked.

Lily told him, "Wish I knew how to write music. That'd be a great song."

Randy laughed, too. "A *country* song, darlin', I haven't changed, but I've slowed down some."

He tried to hum a melody and that made them both laugh.

"The one good thing about me being a sonofabitch?" he said.

"Probably, there's just one."

"Maybe two. The first is, I can say you've always been my favorite. Always will be."

"I stand out in a crowd, huh?"

Randy laughed, and Lily joined him.

"The second thing," he told her, "is you're damn near as crazy as me."

Thinking about the two of them fucking in a cop's bed, she had to agree.

"Tell me another good thing," Lily said.

"Okay. I'm going to get off the rez, make myself a good life, and I'm taking you with me."

Lily said, "Just me?"

"Just you."

Turned out Jackson would go with them, and after Randy had robbed his third bank they had some real money to call their own.

Lily, Randy and Jackson went to Canada first. Let the cops try to find three Indians in all the woods they had up there. But heading north was only a fake-out. They got on a plane in Calgary and flew to Seattle, took another flight down to L.A.

In Los Angeles, Randy bought fake IDs and they took a bus to Flagstaff. In Arizona, they made a cash purchase of a used car and drove to Austin.

Settling in Texas, Randy used most of their money to buy a bar in a Latino neighborhood. There were three rooms in the back where the family could live. Randy became the genial host and bartender. Lily worked as the comely waitress. People liked the handsome couple and their cute little boy. Everyone agreed the new owners were much more simpatico than the old *pendejo* who used to own the place.

The bar prospered and after serving as the site of a wedding reception with a small band Randy got the idea of having live music as a weekend draw. Why not? Everyone else in Austin had live music. It turned out Randy had a good ear, recognized musical talent even at its earliest stages of development. The acts he booked filled the house.

At least once a night, when a band was playing, Randy would step out from behind the bar and take Lily away from waiting tables and lead her out onto the dance floor. People would give them space, whistle, cheer and clap their hands in time with the music.

Lily loved dancing with Randy so much there were times when she'd pull him out from behind the bar. The women all loved her boldness. They all but swooned when Randy took her in his arms at the end of the dance and kissed her.

Jackson often watched his mother and father from the hallway leading to the back rooms, though he was supposed to be asleep. He always sneaked out to listen to at least some of each band's performance. Some he liked better than others, but he loved the idea of making people happy by making music.

Those were the happiest years of Lily's life. She had a larger claim on Randy than any other woman. Not that she had sole possession. At irregular intervals, he would leave Lily and Jackson at the bar with someone he trusted to help with the customers and *go scouting*. Looking to see if any cops had gotten on to them yet, he told Lily.

She knew any cop Randy might spot would be female and the only thing she'd be looking for was a good time. More likely, he had someone special stashed somewhere. When she found out that there was an outside favorite and learned who the woman was she actually approved.

If Randy was going to cheat, he couldn't have made a better choice.

All in all, Lily had to consider herself lucky. For ten years, she had the majority rights to the most handsome man she'd ever known. He'd given her a son every bit as beautiful as he was, had taken her off of the rez, and together they'd made themselves financially secure to a degree they couldn't have imagined as children.

Would have been a wonderful life, if they hadn't had blood on their hands.

If they hadn't gotten their start with stolen money.

Lily came to feel she had to do something to make amends.

The best thing she could think to do was make charitable donations.

She made trips out of town to mail anonymous cash home to Mercy Ridge.

She contributed locally to the families of fallen cops.

When Randy told her he wanted to open a new and bigger place, she said go ahead.

She'd lost interest in the old bar, too, and opened Go Native.

CHAPTER 20

Austin, Texas — July 13, the present

S o who's dead?" Darton asked John, the two of them sitting at his desk in the homicide unit. "Randy or Jackson?"

John said, "We know Randy was a killer. Your department have any criminal record on Jackson?"

"Not a thing, but every bad guy has to start somewhere."

"Maybe coming to Mom's aid?" John said.

"Maybe cleaning up something Mom did. Could be she knocked off the old man when he got to be too big a pain in the ass."

John replied, "Annie Forger described Lily as a wild girl. Willing to be photographed holding on to a Tommy gun. But if Lily and Jackson are alive, where'd they go?"

Darton said, "My guess is not San Diego. How about Cancun? Charlotte Amalie? Somewhere south of the border or in the Caribbean."

John sighed. "That'd cover a lot of ground and water."

"Maybe we could get Coy Wilson to help us. Ask her to listen to small label music CDs from that part of the world. Maybe she'd hear someone using another name performing with Jackson's sound."

John smiled. "That'd be a creative approach. Maybe she could do it by checking music-sharing sites on the Internet. But it would raise the poor woman's hopes for a long-shot hunch, and if it didn't pay off ..."

"Yeah," Darton said. "So, if it's Jackson that's dead, where do you think Randy is?"

"With Lily? Maybe Annie Forger, too, for all we know." John thought about the problem and after a moment began to nod his head.

"What?" Darton asked.

"We might know where to find some answers."

"We might?"

"Yeah, let's head back to Go Native. Have another talk with Barbara Larson."

Inventory had been completed, the store was open and there were half-a-dozen people looking at the wares, two of whom were speaking with the owner. Barbara saw John and Darton enter the shop. She discreetly held her index finger and thumb an inch apart: *Just a minute, guys.*

The customers she was with were a well-turned-out couple and might have represented a big sale both John and Darton thought. Messing that up wouldn't beget an attitude of cooperation, they knew. Darton tapped his wristwatch and drew a circle in the air with his index finger.

Barbara smiled and nodded.

Leaving the store, John asked him, "What was that gesture you made, American sign language?"

Darton laughed. "Heck, no. It was just intuitive. Made up on the spot."

"Meaning what?"

"What do you think?"

"Back in an hour?" John guessed.

"There you go. Wasn't hard, was it?"

"Guess not."

"Hey, I thought you —"

"Don't say it," John told him.

Meaning don't say anything about hand signals being a part of Native American culture. In the interest of law enforcement collegiality, they talked about sports at lunch.

***

Barbara Larson had the store to herself when John and Darton returned to Go Native. She was doing paperwork on a glass countertop. She smiled when she saw them.

"Thanks for the consideration, gents," she said.

"Big sale?" John asked.

"That and more," Barbara replied. "Got myself a consulting job. Going to help deck out a Western-themed restaurant where the idea is authenticity not kitsch."

"Yeah, but will the food be any good?" Darton asked.

"If the chef knows her job as well I know mine, it will."

John said, "That's good, that you know your business so well."

Some of the sparkle left Barbara's eyes; she remembered she was talking to cops, and they were looking for Lily. Her demeanor became businesslike.

"How may I help you?"

John asked, "When you bought this shop, did it come with any encumbrances? Did you assume any debt Ms. White Bird had incurred."

"No, sir," Barbara said. "My daddy warned me about such things, and I've warned my kids. Do not buy things on credit because Mama and Daddy won't be paying off your bills. This place was run at a profit. That's why I bought it. Well, that and I was having a lot of fun here."

"So you took a good look at the store's books?" Darton asked.

"My husband and I both did, looking over our accountant's shoulders."

"There was *nothing* that bothered you?" John pressed.

Barbara pursed her lips — and knew immediately she'd given herself away.

She said, "There had been a loan taken out against the shop, but it had been repaid in full before Lily and I started talking about my buying the place."

John asked, "Did you see what the purpose of the loan was?"

Barbara sighed. "That wasn't in the paperwork, but Lily told me. She took out the loan to keep her husband's bar open. He got behind on paying his liquor distributor and Lily made things right."

John said, "Maybe Ms. White Bird sold her business so she wouldn't have to keep bailing out her husband."

"I already told you I think he was a cheat. The only thing worse than that is an expensive cheat."

When asked, Barbara told them the name of the bar Lily's husband owned.

She said, "It's called Clyde's."

Clyde's was still in business, under new ownership.

"Why didn't Randy Bear Heart call the place Warren's?" Darton asked as they pulled up in front of the bar. John knew what he meant, Warren Beatty, the actor Randy had imitated.

"Clyde's has more snap," he said.

Darton grinned and nodded. They went inside. There were two guys at the bar, one pouring, one drinking. It was the quiet time between lunch and happy hour. Darton handled the badge presentation to the bartender.

"Mr. Hopkins here? We called ahead and he said come on in."

"Boss is in back. Let me give him a buzz and he'll be right out."

The bartender pressed a button on his side of the stick. A moment later, a man in a western-cut suit stepped out of the back room and saw John and Darton. He gestured to them.

"Come on back, boys. Either of you care for coffee?"

The two cops declined. Jerry Hopkins, the new owner of Clyde's, told the bartender no interruptions.

Seating his guests before he sat behind a nondescript desk, Hopkins asked, "What can I do for you gentlemen?"

John said, "We're looking for this man." He placed the photo of Randy Bear Heart and Lily White Bird in costume on the desk. "That was him when he was young."

Hopkins studied the picture and nodded.

"That's John Randall, all right."

"John?" John asked.

"His given name, but everyone called him Randy." Looking at the photo again, Hopkins added, "Hardly seems fair. The man I knew looked more mature but not a whole lot older. Still had the same dark hair, bright eyes and brighter smile. Some folks just don't seem to age."

"You recognize the woman in the picture?" Darton asked.

He nodded. "Randy's wife, Lily. Never met her but Randy had a studio portrait of her in here when I first came to see him about buying the place. She's a fine looking lady. The two of them must've made quite a pair ... when things were still good between them."

John said, "Randy talked about his relationship with his wife?"

"No, he was a gentleman in that regard."

"What other regard is there?" Darton asked.

"The one where a man likes the company of more than one woman."

"He bragged about being a ladies' man?" John asked.

"Not at all, but I do my homework. When I heard about this place being up for sale, I sent some people I trust in to take a quiet look at how it was being run. What they told me, there was a slick fellow who looked to be a ... general manager, you might say. All the other employees, tending bar and waiting tables, were attractive young women. The ladies were real professional with the manager but more than a little friendly with Randy."

"Did you check with the Austin vice squad to see if it had taken any interest in Clyde's?" Darton asked.

"I did just that. The place had a clean bill of health. In fact, it was a regular contributor to the Fallen Officers' Fund. I've kept that tradition going. What I think the deal was, the girls were just girls, looking for the chance to meet a nice young fellow with bright prospects. That and enjoy a romp with the boss every so often."

John said, "If there was no prostitution, how did the slick general manager pad his paycheck? Or was he just looking for someone to marry, too?"

Hopkins laughed. "Julio? No, he was too busy robbing Randy blind."

"How'd you know that?" Darton asked.

"I looked at the books, of course. There was a regular pattern of what Randy described to me as cost overruns. Everything from price increases from the liquor distributor to insurance premiums going up, to utility bills being larger than expected, to … well, you name it. Randy knew all there was to know about showing folks a good time, but nothing at all about minding his cash flow."

John asked, "So how did he keep the place going long enough for you to come along and buy it?"

"He had an angel. Someone with the money to keep the doors open."

"More than once?" Darton asked.

"Twice a year for two years before I took over."

John asked, "You get the idea Lily was his angel?"

"Can't say. All Randy told me was he was selling the place because he was headed for a very comfortable retirement."

"You've got a fella behind the bar now," Darton said. "You let the old staff go?"

"I let the girls go. Julio was gone before I could bounce him."

John said, "Gone how?"

"Can't say about that either, but I did let Randy know Julio was a thief. Maybe Randy sent him on his way with a boot to his backside."

Hopkins told them Julio's last name was Melendez.

"Thing was," he said, "Julio had a Latino name, but you could see he had Indian blood just like Randy did. Could've been why Randy trusted him. Those fellas looked like they could have been family, cousins if not brothers."

CHAPTER 21

Austin, Texas — July 13, the present

Marlene Flower Moon was back in town and met John for dinner at Carmelo's, both of them opting for Italian as a change of pace from Southwestern fare. The meal was on the federal government's dime. Marlene's merlot was out of pocket. John's glass of water was courtesy of the restaurant.

"You've got Gilbert Melvin doing your legwork," Marlene said.

"You mean looking for Annie Forger? Yeah."

"I gave that job to you."

"I re-gifted it," John said.

The day John had started work at the BIA he'd tendered his signed resignation to Marlene. All it needed to become effective was to have a date inscribed on it and to be shuffled in the proper bureaucratic direction.

The document was John's de facto declaration of independence.

He worked his investigations in the ways that made sense to him.

Politics, office or national, be damned.

He had invested the money he had planned to use for his year abroad after college in widows-and-orphans stocks, made regular contributions to add to his holdings and when the money got big enough he swapped everything he had for his first share of Berkshire Hathaway, BRK.A. Warren Buffett had been working hard for him ever since, and now he had two shares.

He also owned a two-bedroom house in Santa Fe, and had

enough money in his checking account that he didn't have to pay any bank fees.

In short, Marlene couldn't threaten him economically.

He said, "I've also got Detective Darton Blake looking for a marriage license and/or divorce decree in the names of John Randall, aka Randy Bear Heart, and Lily White, aka Lily White Bird."

He told Marlene what he'd learned about the fugitives that day.

She gave him a look, wishing she'd had something to hold over him.

Having nothing, she said, "Those are the facts. What do you make of them?"

John said, "Randy killed three cops back in his bank-robbing days. The ways guys like that think, it's okay for them to steal from you but not the other way around."

"So you think —"

"Maybe Randy killed Julio Melendez. Possibly dumped him in Lake Travis. Conceivably saw the possible opportunity to mislead the cops by putting a bit of his jewelry on the body."

"Or maybe Julio killed Randy," Marlene said.

"Could be, if Julio had a history of violence. Darton is looking into that, too. Maybe I'll ask Melvin to take a look at him, as well, in case the FBI or someone else put Julio into witness protection."

Marlene narrowed her eyes, but offered no rebuke.

"What else do you think?" she asked.

"I've been thinking to ask you to find out if Randy Bear Heart had any siblings, maybe a half-brother or even a cousin. That would explain Julio resembling him and why Randy would trust him to handle the money passing through his business."

"Now, I'm working for you?" Marlene asked.

"We're all working together, one big happy family."

She changed directions on him. "You're not staying at the La Quinta now."

"No, I'm not."

She could always find out he'd checked into the Driskill; he saw no reason to make it easy for her.

"You didn't go to Washington this morning," he said.

With Marlene, she might have had a change of planes in Dallas and had decided to circle back. It wouldn't be the first time she'd done that.

"No, I didn't," she said. "I'm going tonight."

"Safe travels," John said. "You still might look into that family angle, though."

Marlene called for their check and put the meals on her business card, tucking the copy of the credit slip into her purse. John had never seen the telltale bulge of a gun in any of Marlene's handbags. He figured her for someone who'd prefer a knife — or teeth — for close-in work.

That was one reason, but not the only one, he'd always turned down invitations to visit her room after business dinners together. Likewise, he always declined the suggestion that he loosen up and drink something with an alcohol content.

Getting to her feet, Marlene asked, "Would you care to tell me where you'll be going with this investigation."

John stood and said, "I'll be leaving town, too."

He didn't elaborate. You never wanted to make things easy for Coyote.

Austin, Texas — July 14, the present

John met Darton the next morning at a diner where a lot of the local cops ate breakfast.

"I'm going to L.A.," he told Darton, "but if my boss or SAC Melvin ask where I am, you don't know."

Darton saluted. "I'll just say you're working an angle you want to keep to yourself."

"That'll work for Melvin. If Marlene asks, just say the damn Injun snuck off before dawn."

Darton grinned. "She likes ethnic humor, does she?"

"Can't get enough. I'll call in if I find something interesting.

Don't leave any notes around. Marlene's great at recruiting spies. I wouldn't be surprised if she already has someone in your office."

"A cop with divided loyalties, imagine that."

The two men shook hands and said goodbye.

It was only when he was on his way to the airport that John thought the slyest move Coyote could have made would have been to enlist Darton.

CHAPTER 22

Los Angeles, California — July 14, the present

John arrived in L.A. in time for lunch and met two Pacific Division traffic detectives at the Cheesecake Factory in Marina Del Rey. It was a beautiful day, sunny and twenty degrees cooler than Texas with a light breeze off the ocean. The three cops decided to dine al fresco.

Toryn Clarke had dark hair, blue eyes and pale skin, looked like she could be the lead in a cop TV show, the seasoned senior officer. Samuel Altschul looked like an academic, but he had the deep tan of someone who spent a lot of time outdoors. He was retired.

John knew why Altschul was putting in an appearance.

He asked both detectives, "First time working with a BIA agent?"

Clarke nodded. Altschul said, "Second."

"Really?" John said. He didn't get that a lot. "You remember the other guy's name?"

"Sure. Couldn't forget it. Marlene —"

"Flower Moon," John finished.

Sometimes there was no eluding the woman, John thought.

"Yeah, you know Marlene?" Altschul asked.

"My boss."

The retired detective smiled. Sympathetically, John thought.

Clarke said, "Probably won't be my last time seeing someone from the BIA. Los Angeles has a growing Native American population."

"Growing population of most kinds," Altschul said.

A waitress brought their lunch orders. After she left they got down to business.

John had called ahead and told Clarke and Altschul about his investigation. They were the detectives who had worked the accident. "I'm coming to think the car crash that killed Vern Forger, Ted Kolchak and Bill Haney was not an accident."

Clarke pulled up the details of the investigation on her iPad.

"The fatalities occurred on the Marina Freeway, twenty-one October, two-thirty-three a.m., temperature fifty-nine degrees, clear skies, no wind, pavement dry with no observed defects, debris or obstructions."

"You have the time pinned down that closely?" John asked.

"As reported by the motorist who witnessed the event and called it in," Clarke said.

Altschul added, "The guy had just dropped off some friends and was headed home. He was his group's designated driver. After calling 911, he got off the freeway, parked and waited for a patrol unit. The officers gave him a field sobriety test and he passed, hadn't been drinking at all. Guy was just a kid, really. Twenty-three. Distraught. Said he'd never seen anything so horrible."

Clarke picked up the narrative. "The car with Forger, Kolchak and Haney was traveling eastbound toward the 405, the San Diego Freeway. It hit a bridge abutment at an estimated speed of ninety miles per hour. Airbags in the vehicle deployed but the ME said the victims died on impact, broken necks all around."

Altschul added, "The abutment got dinged, not for the first time, but it's built to resist major earthquakes. It wasn't close to a fair fight."

Clarke continued reading from her tablet. "Haney had been driving, Forger was in the front passenger seat. Kolchak started out in the back seat, but he hadn't been belted in and was thrown forward on impact, passed between the two front seat airbags and struck the windshield with his head.

"Forger and Kolchak had blood alcohol levels twice the legal limit for driving. Couldn't blame them for that; they weren't driving. Haney was just barely twenty-one, didn't have any alcohol in him, but tested positive for THC."

The active chemical in marijuana.

"Kid never should have been behind the wheel," Altschul said. "The three of them probably never knew what hit them. The witness said there was no attempt to stop. Physical evidence confirms there was no attempt to brake or avoid the abutment."

John sighed and shook his head.

"Yeah," Altschul said. "A lot of these things are head shakers."

The three cops took a break to eat their lunches, and order dessert.

"Anybody notice the smell of dope on the upholstery?" John asked. "Or was there a fire?"

Clarke said, "No fire, but there were three dead bodies and no small amount of blood from Kolchak. Distractions, you know. But I don't remember smelling any marijuana smoke. Do you, Sam?"

He shook his head. "What my former partner and good friend hasn't mentioned ... maybe you'll permit me to do so now, Tory?"

She nodded.

"These fatalities were Detective Clarke's first traffic investigation. She was very thorough, still is. Neither she nor I found any remnants of any alcohol, containers for alcohol, drugs or paraphernalia."

"None of them should have been driving, but there was no sign of anything to cause their impairment?" John asked.

"Only young Mr. Haney *was* driving," Altschul said.

"But there were two professional athletes with him, one sitting right next to him. Even drunk, I'd have to think Forger would have made a grab at the steering wheel when he saw they were going to crash."

The two traffic accident investigators looked at each other and nodded.

"We wondered about that, too," Clarke said.

Altschul added, "Best we could come up with was they'd passed out after entering the vehicle. Kolchak before he could buckle himself in, if that was something he usually did."

"This is speculation," Clarke said, "that's why it's not in the report. But we thought maybe Haney smoked out in the parking lot at the place where his friends had been drinking. The car was a rental. Maybe he thought he'd catch hell if he brought it back reeking of dope."

"You asked around the place where Forger and Kolchak had been drinking to see if anyone had seen Haney smoking?" John asked.

Altschul said, "Of course. Nobody did, and before you ask, his parents said their son never did any drugs. He was too concerned with being in shape so he could be at his best for his hockey games. He was dedicated, they said. We found nothing to contradict that."

Clarke added, "His teammates had trusted him to get them back to their hotel safely."

John asked, "But Haney had spent some time with his teammates while they were drinking, right?"

The L.A. cops exchanged another look.

Clarke said, "Some time. Not all the time."

"Where else was he?" John asked.

"At another table," Altschul told John.

"With anyone else?" John said.

Clarke told him, "Yeah, apparently. What we were told, a number of young women stopped briefly at his table."

"Hookers?"

Altschul shook his head. "It wasn't that kind of place; we checked with vice. Our best guess is, his two married teammates, perhaps joking with a rookie, sent him off to see what kind of ladies he might attract on his own. The club was a place where pro athletes visited regularly, and their presence brought with it —"

"Muscle groupies," Clarke said. "Women who get off sleeping with jocks."

"Jocks who make big money," Altschul added.

"So more than one woman?" John said.

"The best guess we got was three to five," Altschul told him.

"Any helpful descriptions of any of the women?" John asked.

Clarke said, "Big hair, big boobs, tight little dresses: all of them. No names."

John thought about the situation in which young Bill Haney had found himself; then he remembered herbal lore he'd learned from Mom and Dad, and looked at his two counterparts.

He said, "You guys know THC can be distilled, right?"

The waitress refilled the L.A. cops' coffee cups, brought John a bottle of Arrowhead.

"You're saying someone slipped the kid a mickey?" Altschul asked.

Clarke told him, "That's exactly what he's saying. We thought of it, too. Thing is, we couldn't figure out who would do it or why, and how could it have been done without the kid noticing? The stuff would have to taste … well, distinctive. Like dope smoke smells would be my guess."

The son of a *curandera*, John had the answer to that.

"You mask one herb with another. Or with a flower or a bean. Something that's pleasant." He paused to think a moment. "Vanilla beans might be good. Vanilla extract has a high alcohol content, but you probably wouldn't need more than a few drops to spike a drink. Put the distillate in, say, ginger ale, it might not taste bad at all. The kid never would have known what hit him. By the time the blood analysis was done the alcohol could have been gone. Maybe THC persists a bit longer; I'd have to check."

The two L.A. cops stared at him.

Clarke asked, "How do you know all this?"

Altschul pre-empted John. "Marlene Flower Moon knew some strange stuff, too."

I'll bet, John thought. He said, "My mother is a professor of cultural anthropology. She's done a lot of field work. Knows stuff most people don't. Taught me some of it."

"You a doper?" Clarke asked.

"Never touch the stuff." He held up his Arrowhead water. "This is my mainstay."

"You don't drink alcohol either?" Altschul said.

John said, "I like to practice good health habits, and resist stereotypes."

"All right," Clarke said, "it would have been possible for one of the bimbos to doctor Haney's soft drink, if he was drinking anything at all. The question is why would anyone want to do that?"

John knew that Annie Forger had received a windfall, but he phrased his question generally. "Did all three men have life insurance?"

Altschul said, "The kid had what was probably the league minimum, five hundred K. Kolchak had two million, and Forger's policy was getting on into serious money, five million."

"Five?" John asked.

Annie had told him three. Why? Because the larger amount might have made him suspicious?

"Yeah," Clarke said. "He was the star of the bunch, but it went to his wife and she had two small boys to raise."

John looked at the two detectives and said, "Annie Forger, right? What was your impression of her?"

Altschul told him, "Don't have one. She never came here. Word was she was too broken up. Just had the remains shipped home."

"Did the families of the other victims come to L.A.?"

Clarke nodded. "Haney's parents and Kolchak's widow. They were as grief-stricken as any family members we've seen, and we've seen a lot. They'd have given everything they had to have those two guys back."

So it was plausible, at least to Clarke and Altschul, that Annie Forger would have been similarly or even more distraught, what with two young children to care for by herself.

He didn't share his suspicion of Annie with the L.A. cops.

Getting to be just another withholding fed, John thought.
Still, he thanked them for their time and paid for lunch.

Before heading to LAX to find the first available flight to
Vancouver, John had two small chores to attend to. First, he called
Darton Blake in Austin.

"I need a small favor," John said.

"Small favors are my favorite kind."

"I'm going to Canada, unofficially. It'll be easier to do without
taking my duty weapon. Can I send it to you for safekeeping?"

Darton laughed. "Sure. Who's gonna notice one more gun in
Texas?"

John confirmed he had Darton's business address right.

Second, John stopped in at the FedEx location on West Century
Boulevard, close to the airport. He showed his federal ID to a clerk
with a name tag that read Oswaldo. The guy smiled at John.

"Never saw a BIA cred before."

"First time for everything. I want to ship my duty weapon, a
Beretta semi-auto, to the Austin, Texas PD." John took the weapon
out and saw the guy get a little tense. He didn't take offense; no
reason a federal agent couldn't go as crazy as a mail carrier.

Oswaldo relaxed when he saw John make sure the chamber
was clear, drop the clip out of the weapon and pop the cartridges
out. He watched in fascination as John quickly broke the weapon
down and reassembled it minus the firing pin, which he pocketed.

"That was pretty cool," Oswaldo said.

"Something they made us practice in training," John told him.

He pocketed the rounds, too. He'd leave them with an airport
cop.

"I want Priority Overnight on this," John said. He put a personal credit card on the counter.

"You got it. We'll take good care of your weapon."

"Please do."

"Wouldn't want to get in trouble with the government."

"Don't worry about that; worry about my mother."

"Your mother?" Oswaldo asked.

"A sweet woman, but when someone messes with me ... well, in her spare moments, when her temper is up, she's a *bruja*." A witch.

Oswaldo smiled.

"No, really," John said. "Does curses and everything."

Fear crept back into Oswaldo's eyes.

John was sure his weapon would be delivered on time.

CHAPTER 23

Vancouver, British Columbia, Canada — July 15, 2012

John was supposed to let Marlene Flower Moon know if he planned to leave the country while working a case. If he'd been going somewhere distant, say, Europe, Asia or even South America, he probably would have complied. But a neighboring country? That was different. Between John's Athabascan race memory of Canada and the way his parents drifted into and out of Mexico like they were smugglers, there were times he didn't pay more than perfunctory heed to the major borders of North America.

Not that he sneaked into Vancouver. He flew commercial and went through customs. He didn't have his passport with him; he used his BIA credentials as an equivalent travel document. The Canadian immigration officer, a young woman, looked at his ID and asked, "Are you here on business or pleasure, Special Agent Tall Wolf?"

John said, "Thought I'd scout the upcoming hockey season. See how the teams up here are shaping up."

The woman smiled wanly. "If you ask me, most of our best talent plays south of the border these days."

"Mexico?" John asked, kidding her.

She laughed. "Maybe it'll come to that, once Detroit loses its charm."

John got lucky and caught the general manager of Vancouver's pro hockey team in his office. His secretary was fascinated by John's credentials; so many people were. That still might not have been enough to make for a successful cold call, but when John told her he was looking into the deaths of Vern Forger, Ted Kolchak and Bill Haney, he'd said the magic words.

She got on her intercom. A minute later he'd shaken hands with Maurice Satterly and was seated in front of the general manager's desk.

Satterly told John, "It *never* sat right with me, the idea that Bill Haney would have endangered his teammates or himself by driving impaired. That wasn't his nature." Satterly emphasized his point with a shake of his head. "I'm biased, but I just can't see it."

"How biased are you?" John asked.

"I loved that young man like a son, but I never idealized him. I saw him for who he was. I first spotted Bill playing Mite hockey."

John said, "Mite?"

"Three and four year olds."

"You start them young."

"We start with Mini-Mites," Satterly explained. "One and two year olds."

"Wow. Hockey must really be your national passion."

"It is." The GM sighed. "But the game is growing in popularity in your country, Mr. Tall Wolf, and with ten times our population to draw talent from, we've got our work cut out for us."

"So your kids take what they do seriously?"

Satterly said, "The ones who stick with it. Bill Haney was as serious as they come, a dedicated hockey player and a fine young man."

John spotted a signed picture of Haney on the general manager's photo wall. Kid had even had legible penmanship. He was in uniform and was standing next to a woman who looked like she might be his mother.

"Bill have the talent to match his dedication?" John asked.

"Physically, he had enough. Just enough. But he was as hockey smart as anyone not named Gretzky. He knew how to get the most out of his skills. He wasn't ever going to be a superstar, but he inspired all of his teammates to be better just by showing them the effort he put into his game. Someday he's … he would have been a great coach."

John didn't want to let the mood get too blue.

"Vern Forger was a star, though," he said.

Satterly smiled proudly. "Yes, he was. He was an American whose parents had left Canada, but he came home."

"He was a good guy, too?"

The GM nodded. "Him and Teddy Kolchak, both."

"Neither of them would have let Bill do anything foolish?"

"No damn way."

"You ever meet Annie Forger?" John asked.

"I sure did. Nice lady. She and Vern had their two sons born here. The boys have dual citizenship. They're both playing hockey in the U.S. I've kept my eye on them."

"They have pro potential?"

"Yes. Guy a bit more than Louie, but they both could make the league. They come from good stock and have been fortunate to have had good training their whole lives. Ms. Forger has seen to that."

"She's a good mother?"

"Certainly, as far as I know."

John got the impression Satterly had been watching the Forger boys as closely as he'd once watched Bill Haney. Which implied he kept a close eye on other things.

He asked, "Would you know anything about how Vern and Annie got along?"

The GM stared at him. "You really don't think that car wreck was an accident?"

"The more I hear about Bill Haney, the less I believe he chose to get stoned before he got behind the wheel."

Satterly's eyes moistened and he didn't mind that John saw it.

"Then you're the man a lot of people around here have been waiting for, Mr. Tall Wolf. Truth was, Vern and Annie had been having their problems. Seemed the magic had gone out of their marriage. Then her sister came for a visit and things seemed to get worse. I try not to think too hard about the reason for that."

The implication of sibling jealousy, maybe even adultery, was clear.

"Annie Forger has a sister?"

"She did back then. Her name was Lily White Bird."

John was struck dumb. Annie and Lily were sisters?

Lily was maybe just a bit prettier than Annie; he remembered thinking that when Annie had shown him their pictures. But the wigs and berets must have thrown him off, kept him from seeing the family resemblance. Thinking about it now —

"Are you all right, Mr. Tall Wolf?" Satterly asked. "You are going to get to the bottom of all this, aren't you?"

"I'm fine and, yes, I'm going to find out what happened."

John took a room at The Fairmont and set up a conference call with Detective Darton Blake and SAC Gilbert Melvin. He wanted to push things now so he told the two men what he'd learned in L.A. and Vancouver.

Then he asked Melvin, "How do the FBI and the RCMP get along?"

"The Mounties?" Melvin said. "Pretty well. Better than with some of the people on our side of the border."

John said, "If you haven't done so already, SAC Melvin, you want to query Homeland Security, see if Annie Forger has crossed into Canada legally?"

Ms. Forger, John thought, also might move easily across borders without official notice.

Melvin said, "Yeah, I can do that. You think she's headed to Vancouver?"

"She might be a little more subtle than that," John replied. "Her late husband's family came from Quebec. Maybe she entered the country through Montreal."

Darton said, "Maybe she's even holed up somewhere in Eastern Canada. You know, a long way from where she lived as a young wife, and from where she grew up in South Dakota."

Melvin thought of something else. "If she felt a need to go into hiding, maybe the place for her to hide is a Canadian reservation; up there I think they call them reserves. That's the case, getting her out could be politically touchy … and, of course, Special Agent Tall Wolf doesn't do reservations."

"Not even in Canada," John said. "But if it comes to that, I'll ask Ms. Flower Moon for help."

"Better you than me," Melvin told him.

Darton said, "I got some news on Julio Melendez."

"Who?" Melvin asked.

John told him about the guy who'd been robbing Randy Bear Heart at Clyde's.

The FBI man laughed. "There is a God in heaven: the bank robber gets ripped off."

"Yeah, but did Julio get killed for his trouble?" John asked.

"He did," Darton said, "but not by Randy Bear Heart."

"Who killed him?" Melvin asked.

"A Filipino immigrant with a knife. Julio had one, too. The other guy was better. A whole bar full of witnesses said Julio started the fight, just picked the wrong dude. Now, he's buried at county expense in San Antonio."

"I like that, too," Melvin said. "The guy stole blood money from Bear Heart and look what happened to him. Cascading justice."

John said, "Things always worked that way, there'd be damn few people left in the world."

Maybe just a few true followers of the Red Road, he thought.

Them and a lot of buffalo.

"So it's either Randy Bear Heart or Jackson White we found in Lake Travis," Darton said.

"I don't like a kid paying for his old man's crimes," Melvin said.

Thinking of kids triggered a memory for John. "SAC Melvin, you think you could find out if Annie Forger's two boys are still enrolled in college? One's at the University of Maine; the other's at Boston College. Both of those schools are close to Eastern Canada."

Melvin said, "Maine's right next door. Good thinking, Tall Wolf."

John said, "Here's another idea. See if Annie Forger set up trust funds for her sons, made sure they wouldn't want for money."

Annie had told him she wanted to provide for her boys.

Maybe a million each. The difference between the five-million dollar policy on her husband and the three million she'd told him she had.

"I can do that, too," Melvin said.

Amidst all the pleasant feelings of cooperation, John got the sudden notion the FBI man was being too agreeable. He let it go unspoken.

Because he had one idea he hadn't shared.

Not on a three-way call.

John called Barbara Larson in Austin and found her at Go Native.

He asked if she had a moment.

"If I said no, would you let me be?" she asked.

"Sure, assuming you don't want to know how things work out."

She laughed. "You're a smart man, Special Agent Tall Wolf. I wouldn't be human, if I wasn't just a bit curious about all this. Go ahead, tell me what you want?"

John said, "The money Lily borrowed against the store, was that a one-time thing?"

"You mean did that creep of a husband hit her up more than once? Not that it showed on the store's books."

Her answer told John that Randy Bear Heart must have had another source of funds he could tap. Jerry Hopkins, the new owner of Clyde's, had told him that Randy had an *angel* who had bailed him out twice a year for two years running. Having learned all he had about Randy, John would bet that angel was of the female persuasion.

He switched to another topic.

"When we first met and you saw I'm with the BIA, you assured me that all the merchandise in your store had been honestly obtained.

"It was, it is, and always will be. I'm an honest woman with nothing to hide."

John was sorry he hadn't been more tactful, but if you believed John Lennon everybody had something to hide except for him and his monkey.

"I wasn't questioning your honesty, Ms. Larson. I was just wondering if there are less scrupulous dealers who do sell Native American artifacts they shouldn't possess."

"What would your guess be, Special Agent Tall Wolf?"

"I'd say yes."

"You'd be right. Some are almost brazen about it."

John thanked Barbara Larson.

"I'll want to know what happened to Lily," she said.

"Yes, ma'am."

He clicked off.

Now, he had two things to think about: where the sacred objects Randy Bear Heart had stolen might be and who it was that had kept Clyde's afloat before the place had been sold to Jerry Hopkins. Lily had thrown Randy one life preserver.

Had the other financial rescues come from Annie Forger?

Why would she be so generous to a man who had run off with her sister?

Was it likely her generosity had been based on affection and/or sexual gratification?

No, it wasn't.

So what else might Randy have done to earn such solicitude? Maybe play a role in the deaths of three hockey players? That turn of events had earned Annie a five-million dollar death benefit. Say Annie had set aside just one million dollars for her two sons. That would leave her with a million to play with on top of the three million she claimed to have received.

The math worked for John.

So maybe Randy had doubled his body count from three to six.

That night in Canada John had the dream that had haunted him for as long as he could remember. It had occurred with great frequency when he was a young child. His cries of fear would bring both his parents on the run. Mom would hold and soothe him and give him special teas that would ease him back into a peaceful sleep. John wouldn't take the first sip, though, until Dad came back from an armed inspection of the exterior of the house and announce all was well.

The dream was always the same. John was out in the foothills north of Santa Fe, walking in the brush wearing nothing but a pair of shorts. His feet hurt, the soles being too soft for traipsing about without shoes. A nearby growl made him freeze in place. Then the sounds of feet racing toward him filled his heart with panic and broke the thrall.

He ran with all his might and came to a clearing.

There he found a rickety platform and clambered atop it.

No sooner had he stood up than a coyote the size of mountain lion burst into view.

Leaping onto the platform would have been easy for such a beast.

Knocking it over would be easier still.

If either of those things happened, John knew he would be lost.

His only hope was the pile of stones that lay at his feet. He had to hurl them at Coyote and drive him off. It should have been easy to hit such a large target. His arm was strong. He could bloody Coyote, make him pay a high price for frightening John. The problem was, the sun kept getting in John's eyes, not letting him get a fix on the beast.

He threw one stone after another, and he missed each time. His arm was getting tired from the effort. The beast dashed back and forth evading the stones and yipping as if it were laughing at him. When John ran out of stones, it would charge him and he would be lost.

Trembling, he picked up the last stone, and that was when he decided that if his eyes couldn't help him he would use his nose. Squeezing his eyes shut, he held his nose up to the breeze. The scent of Coyote, strong and foul, came to him in a rush.

Told him just where his nemesis was.

He threw the last stone as hard as he could.

His effort collapsed the platform. He fell forward not knowing what his fate would be. Not daring to open his eyes.

He was in mid-air when he heard a howl that froze his blood. He hit the ground hard enough to drive the breath from his body. He could all but feel Coyote's teeth rending his flesh. Waiting for the end was the worst moment.

Then above the pounding of his heart, he heard the beast run off.

Only to stop and howl in anger.

That was the point at which John opened his eyes.

And saw he was in his bedroom.

Rather than feel relief, when he was young, he continued to be afraid, fearing that now Coyote would come for him while he was awake. Being the Trickster, Coyote would find a way to get at him. He'd learn to avoid being struck by any stone that might come to John's hand.

As the years passed and John matured, Coyote showed his cunning by assuming other shapes: sometimes a friend, a classmate, a colleague, an attractive woman in a public place …

Oftentimes Marlene.

Now, the dream came less frequently and, as a man, John was the hunter as often as the hunted. There were still times he found himself at a disadvantage and had to make a narrow escape. That night was one such time. He awoke with a sheen of sweat on his face, sat up in bed and scanned the hotel room with his heart racing.

On the night stand, his cell phone rang.

Answering, he heard Marlene Flower Moon's voice.

Austin, Texas — July 15, the present

SAC Gilbert Melvin, still at his borrowed office, replayed in his head the conversation he'd had with John Tall Wolf and Darton Blake. His two counterparts in law enforcement had been models of cooperation with him, doing their best to keep him fully informed. He'd played along, acceding to Tall Wolf's request to do the scut work the Indian as easily could have done.

At least, he hoped the BIA was up to querying Homeland Security about Annie Forger making a legal border crossing and checking on whether she'd set up trusts for her kids. He had to smile at the way his mind worked. He wanted other agencies of the federal government to be up to snuff in their means and methods, but he wanted them to bow and scrape, defer in every way possible when the FBI put in an appearance.

Melvin thought he must be a royalist.

Or a narcissist.

Either way, he felt good about himself.

Tall Wolf had asked how the FBI got along with Mounties.

Melvin had understated his answer. He had a friend in Ottawa high in the RCMP.

His friend liked to work late, too. Melvin tapped out his phone number and waited for it to ring. He asked himself if he'd done anything to give himself away to Tall Wolf or Blake.

As his call was answered, he decided no, he hadn't.

CHAPTER 24

Vancouver, B.C. — July 16, the present

When John woke up, he wasn't sure whether he'd spoken to Marlene last night or if the conversation had been part of a dream — but he seemed to remember pressing the record symbol on his phone. He was careful about documenting discussions with his boss. He didn't put it beyond the realm of possibility that someday he might be sitting in front of a Congressional committee or a federal judge.

He saw that there was a recording on the phone time stamped 03:44.

He tapped the play symbol and listened to himself answer the phone with a groggy hello.

"What are you doing in Canada?" Marlene asked, sounding irritated.

John heard himself clear his throat and answer, "Promoting international good will and understanding."

He hadn't asked how she knew where he was. Coyote had her ways. His ways?

That was another thing. You couldn't even pin down the Trickster's gender.

"You're supposed to call me before you leave the country on a case."

"Thought I'd be back before you could miss me."

"You are a pain in the ass, Tall Wolf."

This from the woman who had interrupted his sleep.

"You recruited me," John said, "and you keep me on. I must fit into your plans somehow."

Marlene had no comment on that subject. John felt she was about to end the call.

"I could use some help," he told her.

Throw Coyote a bone.

"What kind of help?"

"Would you know of any Indian reserve near Vancouver?"

"First Nation Reserve," Marlene said.

"Pardon?"

"The politically correct term."

"Oh, yeah, that." John remembered having to scratch himself just then. "So, any FNRs near Vancouver?"

"Let me check." John heard the muted click of a keyboard being tapped. No wonder Marlene scared people, he thought, if she could go without sleep all night and hatch her schemes. That and deny other people their rest. "There's a place called Gitlakdamix."

"Easy for you to say." She ignored his drowsy attempt at humor. "Nice place? Eco-tourism outpost maybe?"

"Overlooks a lava flow in the Nisga'a Lava Beds Provincial Park. That might be interesting. But there are only eight hundred residents and the original settlement was destroyed by a flood."

John said, "Mmm." Imagined Marlene tossing him into the lava flow.

He'd try not to let that image crop up in a dream.

"Not what you're looking for?" she asked.

"If Annie Forger is hiding out because she and Randy Bear Heart got back together, I don't see it happening in a place like that. Are there any First Nation resorts up here for local folks who have made good?"

Marlene laughed. "As far as I know, Donald Trump doesn't work with our people."

"He'll get around to it," John said.

Marlene told him, "Regarding another task you set for me, Randy Bear Heart had no siblings, and the only two cousins I was able to locate are both female. Why did you ask that? You thought Julio Melendez might be family?"

At the moment, he couldn't remember whether he'd already told her about Julio or she had found out on her own.

"Yeah," he said. "Thought that might have been a reason Randy had trusted him to handle his money. They were supposed to have shared a physical resemblance."

"Might have been more a matter of character. Attitude."

"Spirit?" John said. "Something beneath the skin that people can still perceive?"

Coyote didn't laugh, but John could imagine that she had smiled.

"Yes, something like that. Call me later today, wherever you are, and let me know if you've found out anything new."

"Abso—" Marlene clicked off before he got to "—lutely."

John hit the stop symbol.

He recalled that as his head had hit the pillow last night he was working on dream management, avoiding any thoughts of heated magma. That was when he'd seen his father's face, and had known that Haden Wolf might be able to help him with his case.

Awake now, he called home.

CHAPTER 25

Austin, Texas — July 16, the present

Coy Wilson went into the room in her house where she and Jackson White used to write their songs. It held two comfortable love seats, a desk, a Baldwin spinet piano that needed dusting, and Jackson's acoustic guitar in its case on a stand in the corner. The guitar case needed to be dusted, too. Whole damn room needed to be cleaned. Had to be five degrees cooler in there than the rest of the house, what with all the dirt on the windows.

Sunlight didn't flood the room, it fought its way in.

Coy sat down at the desk. A pad of paper lay on it, the first line of a song that never got finished was written there in Jackson's boyish but legible handwriting. He'd told her neatness counted. You never wanted to let a great idea slip away because you couldn't read your own writing.

The first line of Jackson's song was:

If I had known it would be like this with you …

That was all. He'd said that was okay because he had the rest of it in his head, and Coy feeling particularly amorous that night had dragged him off to bed. Lily's phone call had dragged Jackson out of bed, and that was that.

No more Jackson, no more song.

She had tried to finish the song on another pad. Never got anywhere with it. Couldn't make it work either lyrically of musically. She wasn't even able to write any new songs of her own. All she had left was the ability to play her own guitar, maybe pick out a basic melody on the piano. She thought even her playing had been affected. Her range was limited compared to the old days. Most of the studio work she did now was bluesy stuff. Everybody said she had a feeling for it that she'd lacked in her younger days.

Anything happy and uptempo, make you want to get up and dance, forget it.

Despite the passage of time, Coy had refused to let go of the last shred of hope that Jackson would come back to her. That Red Hawk would be reborn. They wouldn't be as young as they were when the band should have broken through, but they'd still make it.

Now, after the visit from the cops, she felt sure that Jackson was the one whose body had been found in Lake Travis. She knew it in her soul. The pain was almost enough to keep her in bed all day, but there was also the beginning of acceptance and peace. She would pray for Jackson's soul and let go of her sorrow.

She even saw a ray of hope that her ability to write music might return.

The first thing she did was open the room's closet. She'd long ago stashed Jackson's clothes in there. She patted the dust off the first few items within reach. She checked the clothing for signs of wear and found none. Jackson hadn't been flashy or fixated on designer labels but he'd liked to look good. Someone would be glad to have these clothes. Coy put everything into four boxes to take to the Salvation Army store.

After that was done, she turned to his guitar case.

No way she was donating Jackson's guitar to anyone. It was hers now.

She opened the case and saw that the Gibson Hummingbird gleamed like new; not a speck of dust on it. She took out the guitar and embraced it as if it were her lost love. She could see Jackson's beautiful smile as he played it. No sooner had that image entered her mind than she knew what Jackson would have called the unfinished song.

"If I Had Known."

She saw the verses, bridge and chorus in her mind.

She looked down at the guitar and thought, of course, Jackson must have used it to play the new song, sing the lyrics as he played. The instrument had been patiently sitting in its case just waiting for her to pick it up. If Jackson continued to live anywhere, it was through his guitar.

She'd use it to finish the song, use it and her own six string to write new music. She'd need to tune the Hummingbird and use a capo for "If I Had Known," but —

When she opened the compartment in the case where the capo was kept, she found a key. She took it out and looked at it. There was a number engraved on one side: 2521. On the other side was the name of her bank. It was a key to a safe deposit box.

Her bank had also been Jackson's bank. More often than not, they had gone there together. People mistook them for a married couple, though they had never had anyone but themselves bless their union. They'd talked about making it official … but that was another thing that was never going to happen.

Coy lay Jackson's guitar on the desk. She hadn't known about his deposit box or the key. He'd kept that from her, but why? The only thing she'd left in the closet after removing Jackson's clothes was the box where she kept his unopened mail. She'd left everything sealed. For the first several months after he'd left, there had been mail for him in almost every delivery. After that, it diminished and stopped.

She searched through every envelope. Most of it was junk; none of it was suspicious. She didn't find anything from the bank that looked like an invoice for a safe deposit box. The way she thought that kind of thing worked, a renewal bill got sent out annually.

She called the bank and identified herself as Coy Wilson White. She asked if a payment was due on the box. She was told no, there were two years left on an advance ten-year payment.

Coy took a shot and asked, "Has my husband included my name as a box holder?"

She was told: "Yes, Ms. White, he has."

CHAPTER 26

Santa Fe, New Mexico — July 16, the present

Haden Wolf was at his desk in the clinic when his son called. "Hello, John. How are you? All's well?"

"Doing just fine, Dad. How are you and Mom?"

"No complaints for either of us. We're still fully engaged in life."

Though John and his parents all lived in Santa Fe, his job took him all over the country and on occasions like the current one even out of the country. Mom and Dad were officially retired, but Dad still kept an eye on the free clinic he'd started, and the two of them might disappear for a month or two at a time on what they called scholarly journeys, usually to places where the only roads were unpaved and there were no cell towers whatsoever.

It had been several weeks since John had spoken to either of his parents.

"Still out gathering herbs at first light?" John asked.

"More often than not."

"Find Coyote yet?"

"I had to scare off a mountain lion with a couple rounds last week, but we haven't seen Coyote, no. How about you?"

"Other than my boss, all's clear."

"Your mother and I would like to meet Ms. Flower Moon someday."

John knew his parents' interest was more than just social.

They wanted to see for themselves if their son's suspicions

were accurate.

John didn't want to get into that now.

"Dad, I'm glad I could get in touch. I could use a little medical information." John was sure if his father didn't have the answer to his question, he'd know someone who did.

"What can I tell you, John?"

"Is there a way to determine the age at which a person died from his physical remains, in this case just a skeleton?"

"Sure, there is," Haden said.

John's father told him just how that could be done.

CHAPTER 27

Vancouver, B.C. — July 16, the present

Shortly after speaking with his father, John got an e-mail from SAC Melvin. The FBI man had followed through on John's requests. Guy and Louis Forger, Annie's sons, were still enrolled in their respective colleges and were both training for the upcoming hockey season in Boston. Each of them had a trust fund initially capitalized at five hundred thousand dollars; each fund had grown to just over a million dollars today.

Melvin asked if John wanted him to interview the Forger boys or if he wanted to do it. Maybe with their common Native American ancestry, Melvin suggested, it would be better for John to handle that task. Melvin provided John with an address and a phone number.

Vancouver to Boston was a long haul, but John replied that he would interview Guy and Louis. He went to the Kayak website and found a flight. He could have booked his travel through the BIA. He was supposed to do that so he could get the discount the airlines offered federal employees, but he liked to make Marlene work to keep tabs on him. So he always made his own travel plans. He'd leave Vancouver that afternoon.

Before he left town, he stopped in to see Maurice Satterly again. He now had a few more questions for the man. In response to Satterly's query on the progress of his investigation, John said he was making progress.

The GM wasn't satisfied with that vague description.

"You mean you know something you didn't before?" he asked.

"Yes."

"But you can't or won't tell me what it is right now."

"What I've learned is directional, which way I should move."

"But you think it's the *right* direction?"

"I do."

"You won't cover things up if you find out what happened to Vern, Teddy and Bill?"

"It might not become public knowledge," John said, "but I'll tell you. The information might come with a hold-it-close restriction. You and the Haney and Kolchak families. Could you live with that?"

Satterly sat back in his chair and thought about it. Then he nodded, gave John his mobile and home phone numbers.

"What do you want to know?" he asked.

"Were you surprised when Annie Forger left Vancouver for Rapid City?"

Satterly shrugged. "No disrespect to South Dakota, but I would prefer British Columbia in general and Vancouver in particular."

John didn't take offense; he felt the same way.

Satterly continued, "From what I heard, the Forger boys hated to leave town."

"Vancouver was their home?"

"The only one they'd known. They're Canadian, though they have dual citizenship. This was where they'd lived and started school, and —"

"Where they first put on ice skates?"

"Exactly."

"Did they start as mini-mites?"

Satterly nodded. "Of course. Vern saw to that. The only thing he enjoyed as much as playing the game was teaching his boys to play it."

"Was that part of the trouble between him and Annie?"

"What do you mean?" Satterly asked.

"Well, between playing a full season of hockey, training to get ready for next season and instructing his sons in the finer points of the game, how much time did he have for his wife?"

Satterly got indignant.

"Vern was a good man. It should have been obvious to Annie, should be obvious to any woman who marries a professional athlete, that his sport is where his focus has to be. It's a short career. You have to be dedicated to succeed. You have to be passionate to be great."

"And you told me that Vern was great."

"I did. After their playing days, that's when great athletes have time for their wives."

That sounded to John like a speech Satterly had given more than once.

He didn't doubt that impressionable young athletes took it to heart.

But if you didn't have time for your wife, and you were young and healthy ...

Vern Forger may well have been a good man, but he was human, too, and if there was trouble at home, there was a predictable reason for it.

Taking things a step further, if Vern was having his fun, John could guess where Annie would turn to have hers. Randy Bear Heart. Assuming he was still alive, John didn't see Randy resisting an invitation from one of his two best Bonnies.

Especially if she'd decided to become his angel and help out with his cash flow problems.

Turning to another matter, John asked Satterly, "Do you know if Annie Forger became a Canadian citizen?"

That seemed to be another sore point with Satterly.

"Vern did. It was easy for him, of course. Both of his parents were born here. He fell in love with Vancouver and the city fell in love with him. He decided he wanted to stay. We were all very pleased."

John returned to his question. "Annie didn't feel the same

way?"

Satterly shook his head. "She was content to have permanent resident status."

"Are there any requirements to maintain that status?"

"Yes, you have to spend at least two years of any five year period living in Canada."

"Any exceptions?"

"If you're the spouse of a Canadian citizen whose business takes him or her out of the country."

"Like Vern Forger."

"Before he died, yes."

"One last thing," John said. "Did Annie Forger ever ice skate with her sons?"

"You mean did she take an interest in the game the boys shared with their father? Not as far as I know. I never saw her so much as put on a pair of figure skates."

Satterly made the omission sound like both a crime and a scandal.

"No winter sports at all for her?"

With a lip curled in contempt the GM said, "I heard she liked to ski."

CHAPTER 28

En route to Boston — July 16, the present

On the Air Canada flight to Boston, John made one phone call and received another. Canada, like the U.S., forbade cell phone calls while a plane was in the air. The purported reason for this was that cell phones might interfere with a plane's navigational system. The real reason was that the airlines and a majority of the flying public hated the idea of turning a cramped airplane cabin into a babel of competing conversations.

As with any rule, however, there were exceptions. Two classes of people were allowed to make and receive calls in flight. The aircraft's crew and law enforcement. John had presented his credentials before boarding.

John's privileged standing was enhanced when he got bumped to first class by Madeleine Comfort, a cabin attendant who was also Native American. She whispered that fact into John's ear. He might have guessed regardless.

He wasn't sure, though, that he deserved special consideration.

"Ethnicity," he told Madeleine, "is just an accident of birth."

She said, "Oh, no. Our destinies are planned for us. No accidents involved."

She also told him he should call her Maddie.

Maddie was a tall attractive woman. John did his best not to argue with such people, the exception being Marlene. He tried to see any sign that Maddie might be Coyote. Maybe if he could get her and Marlene into the same room there would be some sign.

"I was hoping you liked my mysterious good looks," John told Maddie.

The first class compartment was sparsely populated. Didn't see that much in the U.S., but it made for easier flirting.

"What I'd like is a peek behind those sunglasses," Maddie said.

John lowered the Ray-Bans to the tip of his nose.

Maddie must have liked what she saw because the service was exceptional, his maybe a bit better than the others in first class.

The call John made was to SAC Melvin. He told the FBI man of his conversation with Maurice Satterly, and mentioned that Annie Forger had permanent resident status in Canada.

"What I've been thinking," John said, "is that Annie got five million dollars from the life insurance policy, but she also must have inherited an estate of some size. Vern Forger had to be making a small fortune as a star athlete."

Melvin said, "Yeah. Not as much as a baseball or basketball player, but real nice money compared to your average government employee."

John laughed. "So, anyway, if Annie wants to keep her permanent resident status in Canada, and I bet she does, she probably has a house up there. You think you could find out where?"

"Sure, but you could, too, if you wanted."

"You saying we should stop sharing?" John asked.

"No, it's kind of refreshing. Makes me wonder what could be accomplished if everyone cooperated."

"Yeah, so, you'll check it out?"

"Uh-huh. Find Ms. Forger's Canadian digs."

"You have anything I should know?" John asked.

"Would have told you by now," Melvin replied.

But there had been half-a-beat of hesitation before he answered. And his goodbye was just a bit rushed.

Which left John wondering just what the FBI man was holding back.

John turned down a champagne cocktail from Maddie in

favor of sparkling water. She saw he had something on his mind and didn't linger to chat. Consideration. A good move for both the kind hearted and the calculating. But John didn't have time to classify Maddie at the moment.

He was thinking of how much he should share with Melvin from now on.

Not everything, of course. But if he cut him off completely, Melvin would stop running John's little errands for him, and he liked the idea of having the FBI act as his time saver.

Before he could decide just how to play things, his ring tone sounded.

Darton Blake was calling.

The detective started the conversation by asking John, "Do you watch much television?"

"Hardly any."

"Other than sports, I'm the same. Maybe we're missing something that way."

"Like what?" John asked.

"Well, there are these science based mystery shows and —"

John knew right where Darton was going.

"They can tell you how old someone was when he died," he said.

John listened to the jet engines thrum as Darton fell silent.

He continued, "They look at things like teeth, ribs, face structure and a lot of other stuff. You put it all together you get an accurate reading on the age at time of death."

Darton jumped right back in now. "How'd you know that? How'd you know I was going to tell you that?"

"Guessed," John said.

But it had been an intuitive guess. Something he'd felt.

"You *guessed* how they work out a body's age at time of death?"

"No, I guessed what you were going to tell me. My father told me about the details; he's a doctor. I thought he might know, so I called him."

"Huh. Looks like we had the same idea."

"Who'd you talk to, seeing that you don't watch TV."

"The anthropologist who worked the crime scene at Lake Travis."

"Her report came in and you read it?" John asked.

"I called her and she told me."

John needed only a second to understand what that meant.

"Melvin got the report first. He already knows whose body went into the lake, and he's been holding out on us."

That was the reason for the hesitation John had heard from the SAC.

"You're spoiling all my fun," Darton said. "Technically, Melvin wasn't holding out. He just fixed things so he got the information first and it's available to us upon request."

"So who's dead?" John asked. "I think I can guess, but I don't want to."

"Jackson."

"Damn."

Darton felt the same way. "Yeah. It would have been better if our murdering bank robber had been Mr. Bag o' Bones."

John brought Darton up to date on his end of things.

"Thanks," the detective said, "I'll know better now than to distrust all you feds."

"Best to remain somewhat skeptical," John advised and said goodbye.

Thirty minutes before landing in Boston, Maddie asked John if he'd have any free time after they touched down. He said he was busy, but he thought he'd be visiting Canada again soon.

"Really? Where are you going?"

In the way cops often responded, he answered her questions with a question.

"Well, if you like to ski in the winter and, say, hike in the summer, and you have plenty of money, where in Canada would you live?"

Without hesitation, Maddie told him, "Banff."

John said, "That might be the place."

— 134 —

CHAPTER 29

Austin, Texas — July 16, the present

A s John's flight was taking off for Boston, Coy Wilson arrived at the bank with her heart in her throat. She felt as if she was going to rob the place not access a lock box to which she had the key. Still, she would be posing as Jackson's wife. Well, who the hell knew, she thought. As long as they'd lived together, maybe under Texas law she had qualified as a common law wife. The thought reassured her, somewhat.

If that wasn't enough, Jackson had put her name down as someone entitled to get at whatever the box held. She wondered if he ever intended to tell her about what he'd hidden in there. Maybe it was something he'd wanted her to see only after he …

Well, hell, chances were he was dead.

The lady who handled the paperwork for getting a box out of the vault was perfectly courteous with Coy. That calmed her down a little more. When it came time to sign her name, to show she'd been given access to the box, she wrote Coy Wilson White.

Anybody looking at the signature afterward wouldn't be able to say she was trying to pose as someone else, and she'd be able to say she considered herself Jackson's wife. She didn't know if that would mean anything legally, but she thought it might give a lawyer grounds to defend her. Give a sympathetic juror reason to acquit.

"Will you need a room for privacy?" the bank lady asked after pulling the box out of the vault wall.

"Yes, please," Coy said.

No way was she going to open the thing in front of anyone else.

The bank lady didn't bat an eye. No big deal to her. But now that Coy held the box in her hands her heart was hammering again. Not only did she think she might find something shocking, she felt as if she might be opening a coffin. Christ, what if someone had put a *part* of Jackson in the box?

It was a crazy thought, but Jackson's disappearance was nuts, too.

Now finding this damn box … she was glad it was too small to hold a head.

"Just press the buzzer and I'll be right back," the bank lady said.

That was when Coy first took notice that she'd followed the woman into a small windowless room, seated herself and put the box down on a counter in front of her.

"Thank you, I will," Coy said.

The woman closed the door behind her. There was a lock button in the doorknob. Coy pushed it. Secure and alone, she still needed a minute of looking at the box before she could open it. Even then, she had to remind herself that she'd always trusted Jackson's judgment.

She took a deep breath and lifted the lid.

The first thing she saw was a glassine sleeve with strips of developed 35 mm film inside. Next to the film was a number ten envelope. Jackson's name was inscribed on it in a feminine hand. Both the sleeve holding the film and the envelope rested on a bed of cash.

Coy had imagined that she might find some money but nowhere near what she saw. Banded packs of hundred dollar bills, all of them looking mint fresh, filled the bottom of the box. Stamped on the band of each pack was the figure $10,000. There were ten packs.

In addition to performing with Red Hawk, she and Jackson had both been working studio musicians. They had made a comfortable living, but not nearly as much as they might have if they hadn't invested half their time and almost as great a part of their income on the band. No way had they made enough for Jackson to stash a hundred grand. Certainly not without Coy noticing that maybe they hadn't eaten for the past year.

She picked up the sleeve holding the film. She recognized the pictures. They had been shot by a photographer friend, poses she and Jackson had struck with the idea one might become the cover art for their first Red Hawk album. Seeing the images now made Coy's eyes sting. She put the exposures aside.

She picked up the envelope with Jackson's name on it, looked at the handwriting. It was definitely the work of a woman. But there was no perfume on the envelope. No lipstick kiss to seal it. It didn't strike Coy as anyone's idea of a love letter. As far as she knew, Jackson's mom was the only other woman in his life. Before Coy opened the envelope, she looked at the door to the room. The lock button in the doorknob was still depressed. The door was squarely in its frame. There was no telltale sound of anyone standing just outside.

Coy took a nail file out of her carry bag and neatly slit the envelope open. She took out a single sheet of white typing paper. On it, written in the same hand that had inscribed Jackson's name was ...

Coy's eyes flew across the message. It was signed Lily White Bird. Jackson's mom.

She had confessed to killing her first husband, a tribal police officer.

Named Daniel Red Hawk.

Coy stifled a sob, thinking, Oh, Jesus, did you know about this, Jackson?

Was this how you came up with the band's name?

Was this the reason you disappeared?

CHAPTER 30

Boston, Massachusetts — July 17, the present

John had gotten into Boston late enough the night before that he hadn't wanted to head straight to the Forger brothers' house. Knock on someone's door after reasonable visiting hours, they'd have a good reason for telling you to get lost. He took a room at the Charles Street Inn. The staff there was patriotic enough to give him a government discount and sophisticated enough not to say they didn't get many guests from the BIA.

John didn't know Boston but he knew swank when he saw it the following morning. The North End townhouse where the Forger brothers lived had been rehabbed to a magazine layout gloss. If the place wasn't a rental, then trust fund assets weren't the only big money the boys had to their names — though John guessed that if the property was in anyone's name, it was Annie's or that of a holding company she controlled.

He pressed the doorbell, didn't hear a ring or a chime, but a moment later a young man who stood about six-two opened the door. He had to look up to meet John's eyes.

John showed the kid his federal ID.

"You're one big Indian," the kid said. "A red man in Ray-Bans."

John laughed. "You like being politically incorrect?"

"Pretty much. Still, with you, it's cool."

"How's that?" John asked.

"Well, just between us Native Americans, I've got tribal license. You know, the way African American people can use the n-word."

John said, "Learn a new thing every day. May I come in?"

"Sure. Wait, you're not here to arrest anyone, are you? *Can* you arrest people?"

"I can, but all I'd like to do is talk with you and your brother."

"About?"

"Your father among other things."

The kid smiled. Got a little choked up, too.

"Always happy to talk about Dad. Come on in. I'm Guy Forger."

He used the French pronunciation, too.

Guy stepped aside, allowing John to enter. Sitting on a sofa in the living room was another young man. He put the book he'd been reading on a coffee table. John saw the cover: *Down to My Last Dime*. Below the title was a photo of a handsome gray-haired African American man.

John knew of the author and his story. Albert Winston had been a former NBA player, had been kicked out of the league for drug use and at bottom literally had ten cents left to his name. Nonetheless, he managed to turn his life around and start a self-help organization called Last Best Chance.

Cautionary reading for any young athlete, John thought. Especially one born into the first generation of privilege whose forebears had known nothing but hard times. That kind of self-awareness told John he'd be dealing with more than just a couple of jocks.

"That's my brother, Louie," Guy told John.

John shook his hand and asked, "Good book?"

"Makes you think, that's for sure."

"This is Special Agent Tall Wolf, Louie. He's with the BIA."

Louie smiled. "Yeah? Can I see?"

John showed Louie his ID.

Guy said, "He can arrest people."

"Even white people?" Louie asked. "Boston Brahmins?"

"White, black, brown, red. Rich or poor. I don't discriminate," John said.

"But not us and not now, right?" Louie asked.

"Right."

Guy said, "Have a seat, Mr. Tall Wolf. You want something to drink?"

John sat in an arm chair and said, "Spring water is always good."

Guy plopped down on the sofa next to his brother and nudged him.

"Get the man a Poland Spring, okay?"

Louie nodded and got to his feet. "You want one, too?"

"I'm good."

Louie nodded and left the room. John sensed the respect he had for his older brother.

"You've stood up for him a time or two, haven't you?" John asked.

Guy shrugged. "Whenever it was called for; he does his own heavy lifting now. What kind of questions you got?"

"Personal ones, I'm afraid. If it's okay with you, I'd like to ask about your mother first."

Guy was thinking about that when Louie returned with an unopened bottle of water. He gave it to John and sat next to his brother.

"He wants to talk about Mom," Guy told Louie.

"That's okay by me."

John was happy to hear that; glad, too, the seal on the water bottle hadn't been broken. You never knew when people might want to tamper with your drink — maybe slip some THC into it. He twisted off the cap and took a sip.

Guy hadn't seconded Louie's approval yet, so John went another way.

"You guys are old enough to remember your father, aren't you?"

Guy said, "Sure."

Louie said, "He's a little fuzzy to me. I thought we were going to talk about Mom."

"If it's okay with your brother," John said.

Guy nodded. "Yeah, I guess. Go ahead."

"As far as either of you can remember," John said, "did your parents get along with each other?"

"They didn't fight in front of us, if that's what you mean," Guy said.

Louie shrugged. "They were just there is all I can tell you."

"Do you remember if they were affectionate with each other?"

"You mean huggy-kissy?" Guy thought about that. "Anytime Dad came home from a road trip, we all greeted him at the door. He'd grab Louie and me and pick us up, both of us together."

Louie brightened. "Hey, I remember that! Yeah, that was really cool. The way I felt with Dad holding us, it was like he was the strongest man in the world."

"He was strong," Guy said.

"Did you father hug your mother, too?" John asked.

Guy told him, "Yeah, he did. He'd put us down and throw an arm around Mom and plant a good one on her."

"A kiss?" Louie asked.

Guy nodded.

"Don't remember that," his brother told him.

John asked Guy, "Were you able to tell if your mother was as happy to see your father as he was to see all of you?"

Guy's face showed suspicion, but he said, "She kissed him back. What else is …" The childhood recollection caught up with what Guy had come to know of women as a young man. "You know, maybe Mom wasn't quite as happy as …" Further understanding occurred and Guy shook his head. "I don't think either of them was all that happy. Not as much as either of them was happy about being with Louie and me."

A look of sadness filled Louie's eyes.

"Maybe Mom liked to be with us when we were little, but how much time has she spent with us in the last ten years?"

John wasn't going to ask the two young men if they thought their mother had been having an affair while their father was still alive and playing hockey away from home. Things had reached a point that was delicate enough already. He might not get many more answers.

He went in another direction.

"After your father died, did your relationship with your mother change?"

Guy rolled his eyes. "She moved us to South Dakota. We begged her not to."

"That's what I was just getting at," Louie said. "We didn't have to stay in Rapid City long."

"Why not?" John asked, surprised.

Louie told him, "We got sent to boarding school in Pomfret, Connecticut."

"Really good school," Guy said, "and equally good hockey team."

Louie said, "Thing was, Mom used to come and visit all the time up 'til Guy reached high school. After that, it was just Christmas and Easter."

After that, John felt sure, was when Guy became his brother's surrogate parent.

"What about summer vacation?" John asked.

"Mom came for a week," Guy told him. "We'd go to Manhattan, buy stuff, see some movies, maybe a play. After that, it was goodbye and we were off to hockey camp."

"Otherwise, we just had phone calls," Louie said.

There were other personal questions John might have asked but he felt he'd spread enough gloom. He had just one more thing he wanted to know.

"Does your mother have a house in Canada?"

Guy nodded. "Yeah, she rents a place in Banff."

John took a calculated risk. He called a cell phone number Guy had given him. Annie Forger answered on the first ring. There was no reason she shouldn't have. He was calling from her sons' home phone.

"Guy?" Annie said.

"No, Ms. Forger, this is John Tall Wolf calling."

There was a moment of silence. John thought she might hang up on him. That would be all right. The simple fact that he'd called from the Boston town house sent a message. But Annie Forger stayed on the line.

"What do you want?" she asked.

Smart woman, John thought. She might as well see if she could learn something to her advantage.

John said, "There were skeletal remains found in Lake Travis in Austin, Texas this week. They were identified as belonging to your nephew, Jackson White. He might be thought of as Jackson Bear Heart, though, as he was Randy's son."

"That's terrible," Annie said.

"Yes, it is. But you don't sound too surprised or upset. Lily must have told you what happened."

"What's your point, Mr. Tall Wolf?"

"My point is, I'm on my way to see you. The FBI will be there shortly, too, assuming Randy Bear Heart is with you and your sister. Don't think being in Canada will help you. We'll have the Canadian authorities with us. If you run, I'll find you."

"Lily and I haven't done anything wrong," Annie said.

John ignored the denial. "I advise you to have a lawyer on hand when I arrive."

He was the one who ended the call.

Guy and Louie had listened on an extension. Louie looked like he might say something. Guy put a hand on his arm to silence his brother.

John let himself out.

CHAPTER 31

Banff, Alberta — July 17, the present

"You want to go on a picnic?" The idea took Randy Bear Heart by surprise.

He was still in bed, had opened his eyes only thirty minutes ago. Usually, Lily and Annie gave him an hour to himself after waking. Or one of them would slip under the covers with him for a morning frolic. It had been a while, though, since all three of them had a go at it.

That was what Lily had just proposed. Outdoors yet.

Randy didn't kid himself that he was the young stud he used to be.

He couldn't imagine robbing a bank these days.

Almost found it hard to believe he had ever done so.

But he still had that old killer smile.

The question was, would he be able to satisfy two women in quick succession? He glanced out the bedroom window. It was a beautiful morning. Sunny. The mountains stood in knife sharp relief against the bright blue sky. Still, a patch of grass, even with a blanket, was no match for his Serta Perfect Sleeper. Sometimes his back could act up.

"How about we just open the window?" Randy asked.

Lily scowled. "Annie's fixing a picnic basket. I'll tell her to forget it."

Randy held up a hand to stop her. "Outside? Out-damn-side?"

"You used to like it."

Yeah, Randy thought. I liked it anywhere. Only now I like my comfort, too.

That thought made him realize: He *was* getting old. Swinging his feet off the bed, he said, "My back gets sore, you'll give me a rub?"

"We'll rub any ... thing ... you ... want."

Randy smiled, feeling younger by the moment.

He'd show Lily and Annie what he could do.

"I'll shower and be right down," he said.

Lily White Bird and Annie Forger took Randy Bear Heart to an alpine glade five miles outside of town. The day had grown even more glorious. The sun was warm but a soft breeze carried a breath of coolness. Yin and yang were in the air. The hikers felt both relaxed and energized. Randy was so eager he took the lead from the parking lot where they'd left their car.

He huffed and puffed a bit as the trail climbed.

The two sisters followed, Annie carrying a large wicker basket.

Three times on the ascent Randy saw a place that would have suited him. "This is it, right? How about here?"

"Not here," Lily told him.

"The far side of the mountain," Annie said.

Up beyond where any tourists would go.

Wouldn't want to put on a show for the public.

Randy leered. He'd had each woman more times than he could remember, but what always kept him interested was that each time was a *new* time. It never got old for him.

Randy said, "I hope you got all sorts of goodies in that basket. I'm working up a *big* appetite."

Annie smiled. "I brought everything we'll need."

"I'm a happy man," Randy said. "I'm glad you talked me into this. Climbing to the top of a mountain with my two best Bonnies."

Spurred by that happy prospect, Randy picked up the pace. Annie and Lily looked at each other. It was a moment when they might have reconsidered what they were about to do. But they nodded to each other and pushed on.

When Randy reached a turn in the trail and saw a staggering view of neighboring peaks stretching off the north, he knew he'd reached their destination.

"This *has* to be it," he said.

The site was a large green outcrop that extended from the side of the mountain. The trail ended there. At the far edge was a drop-off that might have made a mountain goat queasy. In an act of predestination, Randy carefully stepped to the brink and peeked into the abyss.

He stepped back before he lost his balance.

"The view is great up here, but we better not roll around too much," he said, turning to look at Lily and Annie.

Each of them was wearing a blonde wig and a beret. Lily had Randy's old Thompson submachine gun. The weapon had been in hiding all those years, too, but Lily had retrieved it. Randy wanted to think this was all a joke. Part of the deal to get him worked up. Make him think he was Clyde again. Maybe they'd brought his hat for him and —

Self-deceit lasted only until he looked into Lily's eyes and understood how those two cops he'd killed must have felt when he put the Thompson on them. He raised his hands like a man who was being robbed, and he was. His last chance to live had just been taken from him.

All he could ask was, "Why? Why now?"

"You killed my son," Lily said.

"And Guy and Louie barely know me," Annie added.

Randy protested, "Jackson was going to turn me in to the cops. When I tried to take the phone from him, I had to fight for my life. It was only luck I was able to grab that ax."

"Bad luck, the way it turns out," Lily said.

"You said you forgave me."

"I thought I had," she told him. The Tommy gun said otherwise. Her finger was on the trigger.

Desperate, Randy turned to Annie. "Why are you doing this?

You don't know your boys, get to know them. And don't forget I hired the hooker to spike that kid's drink. *I* made you rich."

Annie said, "And I repaid you, the times I bailed you out at Clyde's, the times I took you to Vegas when you just had to get away from Lily. If I'd forgotten about you when I married Vern, I might have been a good wife, made my husband happy, wound up rich anyway."

Randy's expression hardened. "There's nothing good about either of you. You're just a couple of whores."

Lily said. "That's the point. We are women of damn poor character and judgment. You can get us to do things we should never do, but we're always foolish enough to give you one more try. Even when we should know better."

Annie told him, "We thought this time the two of us together might finally be enough for you, but we're not altogether stupid. From the moment we set foot in Banff, we had a private investigator following you. We know about all the other women you've had here. Tourists and locals."

Randy was dumbfounded. Then amused to the point of laughter.

"*That's* what's bothering you? You thought I was going to *change?* You *know* who I am."

Annie said, "Yeah, we know. But something else has finally changed. There's this smart Indian tracking us now. If we get connected to you, we become your accomplices. We go down for everything you've ever done. So, baby, the time has finally come to say goodbye."

Randy knew there would be no appeal for mercy.

He got one step into an attempt to flee when Lily pulled the trigger.

The hail of bullets roared past Randy, inches to his left. He responded in the only way possible; he backed up as fast as he could. His second step carried him to the edge. His arms wind-milled, he fell and he screamed all the way down.

Not so much as nicked by a single round.

As Annie had said, she and Lily weren't altogether stupid.

If Randy's body was recovered anytime soon, it would be found pulped but not perforated. He'd be adjudged the victim of an accident or suicide.

Lily put the Tommy gun back into the picnic basket, along with the blonde wigs and the berets. The two sisters, each occupied by her own thoughts and regrets, started down the mountain in silence.

CHAPTER 32

En route to Calgary — July 17, the present

John flew Air Canada from Boston to Calgary. Maddie Comfort, the friendly cabin attendant from his trip east, wasn't working this flight and he had to fly coach. He got a bulkhead seat, though, the solicitous crew showing concern for his height and, possibly, his position with the U.S. government.

The flight was smooth, the kind that made John think an experience like this gave people the idea they were meant to fly. Just sit back and look out the window at the sunlit checkerboard of golden clouds and blue sky and hope that any afterlife might have views half so grand.

There were those people, his parents included, who studied cloud formations for portents of the future. Most of those people had seen clouds only from below. For all they knew, the true meaning of clouds might be revealed only from above. John peered down to see if that might be the way of it.

He saw all sorts of shapes: animals, insects, even an old teacher or two. He didn't know that they told him anything about the future. Maybe, he thought, clouds were only reminders of things already perceived and stored in memory. Flashcards in the sky.

Then, an hour into the flight, the lowering sun now giving the sky a reddish cast, he saw in a cloud a face he had never seen in life but only in a photograph: Daniel Red Hawk. Lily White Bird's late husband. The reservation cop Randy Bear Heart was said to have killed.

The detail of the face in the cloud, John thought, was extraordinary, as though a gifted draftsman had rendered it. Frederick Remington maybe. What was equally compelling was the face's expression. Red Hawk was smiling broadly.

It seemed almost as if he was telling John, one cop to another, this case was going to work out for the best. Justice would be had for Randy Bear Heart … and maybe for his former wife, if she'd been complicit in his death.

Had Lily set up Red Hawk to be killed?

Suddenly, John wanted to be on the ground in Canada.

Driving to Banff as fast as he could.

CHAPTER 33

Austin, Texas — July 17, the present

Detective Darton Blake was about to get into his personal car and go home when he heard a horn honk. He looked in the direction of the sound and saw a Volkswagen CC sedan pull up in front of him. Coy Wilson was behind the wheel. That made him smile. Back in the day, a musician like Coy would be driving a VW bug or a minivan, if she were about to go out on tour. Now, here she was with a gleaming thirty-thousand-dollar ride. Times sure had changed.

The mirth Darton was feeling disappeared when he remembered that Coy hadn't heard the remains in Lake Travis had been identified as Jackson White. Shit. He'd hoped to get home in time to have a hot dinner, but now he had the feeling he wasn't going to feel like eating at all.

He walked over to Coy wondering whether he should put off telling her until tomorrow. He nodded and said, "Hello, Ms. Wilson. Something I can do for you?"

She handed him a cloth shopping bag from a Central Market store. Its weight surprised Darton, but not half as much as what he saw inside: stacks of banded cash.

"You rob a bank, Ms. Wilson?" Darton asked.

Coy told him, "The money came from a bank, but I didn't steal it." She told him about finding the lock box key and going to see what Jackson had kept in it. "I don't know where that money came from, but if it's from something bad, I don't want any blame for having it."

"How much is it?" Darton asked.

"One hundred thousand dollars, exactly. On the other hand, if the money was made honestly, I'll want it back. All of it."

"Yes, ma'am. If you'll just come inside, I'll impound the money, write up your statement and give you a receipt."

She looked to Darton's eye as if she was trying to fight back tears. Whether that was because of handing over so much money or imagining the bad ways Jackson White might have come by it, he couldn't tell.

She surprised him when she said, "There's nothing more to say than what I already told you. You can mail me the receipt." As if to underscore her faith in him, she added, "I'd appreciate it if you returned my shopping bag, too."

That was when the news Darton had been holding back popped right out of his mouth. "Ms. Wilson, I'm sorry to tell you the remains found in Lake Travis were those of Jackson White."

She only nodded, as if she'd come to that conclusion on her own.

Unable to hold back her tears any longer, she drove off.

Watching her go, Darton thought he should have asked her if she'd found anything else in that lock box. Too late now. He took the money inside, thinking at least he'd have a good story to tell his wife, why he was late for dinner.

Then he thought he'd better tell John Tall Wolf the story, too.

CHAPTER 34

Calgary, Alberta — July 17, the present

John didn't know what the fine for speeding on a Canadian highway might be, but he was sure he didn't need the hassle of a traffic stop. He called the RCMP from the plane and upon reaching Calgary received assistance in the person of a uniformed sergeant. Rebecca Bramley stood at parade rest as the stream of deplaning passengers parted ways for her. At six-one she had no trouble spotting the man wearing sunglasses and holding a carryon bag who ducked his head coming out of the jetway.

She stepped forward and asked, "Special Agent Tall Wolf?"

John nodded and Sergeant Bramley introduced herself.

He extended his hand and said, "Thanks for the help."

Taking his hand, she said, "The force is always happy to assist a colleague."

"*Maintiens le droit,*" John replied. Defend the law. The RCMP motto.

"*Exactement.* You've worked with us before?"

"Haven't had the pleasure. But I thought it would be polite to learn a thing or two about the people who were kind enough to lend a hand."

Bramley inclined her head, indicating the way to her car.

"You Googled us, Special Agent."

He fell into step with her. "I did. Please call me John."

"Thank you. Your French accent is quite good, John."

"I went to a terrific college."

"Well, good for you." They stepped outside. A Ford SUV with RCMP markings and a light bar stood at the curb. "Here we are."

Before going to the driver's side, the sergeant cast an appraising look at John.

"Something wrong?" he asked.

"You needn't have ducked your head as you stepped into the airport, but you might be a little cramped in my car, even with the seat pushed back all the way."

"I'll try not to complain … unless you play country music all the way to Banff."

Bramley smiled at him. "I could, but I like alt rock, too."

"Much better."

"So what kind of bad guy are we looking for?"

"Bank robber. Left three dead behind him."

The sergeant's face tightened. "Damn. With a guy like that, maybe we'd better pound some heavy metal into our heads."

CHAPTER 35

Banff, Alberta — July 17, the present

Annie Forger and Lily White were dining in a Southwestern themed restaurant on Caribou Street. Annie started out with corn tortilla and chicken soup. Lily chose an oven baked quesadilla. Their newly hired lawyer, Colin McTee, sat with them. The sisters had offered to buy dinner for McTee but he'd contented himself with a glass of lemonade.

After disposing of Randy Bear Heart and taking other precautions, Annie and Lily had called on McTee. The lawyer had made news the previous year by winning an acquittal for a French actress accused of killing an Austrian director in the chalet the two had rented for the ski season. McTee had created reasonable doubt in the minds of the jury by casting suspicion on a jealous ski instructor whose whereabouts were currently unknown.

McTee had been about to leave town for a fishing trip in British Columbia, but Annie Forger had presented him with a check for his standard retainer and told him she and her sister needed his help, but if he was as good as everyone said they wouldn't need much of his time.

"What's the problem?" McTee asked.

"Poor choice of a boyfriend," Lily told him.

The lawyer smiled. "That often leads to trouble. Who wants to talk with you?"

Annie said, "The RCMP, the FBI and the BIA."

McTee was familiar with the first two but not the third.

"Bureau of Indian Affairs," Lily told him. "That's the one that worries us."

Annie added, "Special Agent John Tall Wolf. He's the one who advised us to get a lawyer."

McTee said, "I suspect I may be assisting you longer than you think. But I'm intrigued. This boyfriend, you were both infatuated with him?"

The sisters nodded.

"Is he likely to provide testimony that might be incriminating to either or both of you?"

Annie and Lily looked at each other. Lily said, "He's been avoiding the cops for a very long time. I don't think he's going to come forward now."

"Good. When do you think the authorities might arrive to question you?"

Annie said, "Could be any time."

McTee said he would remain with them until they cleared that hurdle.

Annie and Lily both ordered the blue corn chicken enchilada for their main course. McTee broke down and asked for the barbecue chorizo flatbread. They were all enjoying their meals when SAC Gilbert Melvin and Superintendent Manley Kent found them. They were reinforced by two RCMP uniformed constables.

Kent handled the introductions for himself and Melvin.

The two cops remained anonymous.

Annie asked, "Where's Tall Wolf?"

Kent looked at Melvin for an explanation.

Melvin had his own question for Annie. "You talked to him?"

"Yeah. He made it sound like he'd be here first; you guys were just back up."

Melvin's jaw tightened as if to bite back a curse. Then he told Kent, "The BIA guy I told you about. I didn't think he'd get here for a while."

Kent stepped forward. It was his country, whatever the squabble the Americans had amongst themselves. "Would you oblige me with a few formalities?" he asked the sisters. "You are Annie Forger and Lily White Bird?"

McTee stood and said, "I'll be speaking for my clients."

"They feel the need to invoke their right to silence?" Kent asked.

The superintendent and Melvin had flown out from Ottawa after his friend from the FBI had located Annie Forger's whereabouts and explained to Kent the necessity of interviewing her. The superintendent had heard of Colin McTee, but was far from awed by the provincial lawyer. If anything, he thought McTee should be deferential to him.

As in the U.S., however, Westerners in Canada could prove both ornery and independent.

McTee told Kent, "My clients wisely seek to protect their rights from overreach by authorities both domestic and foreign."

The faces of both senior cops turned flinty.

Kent looked at the plates of food on the table in front of him.

"Will you be ready to speak for your clients after they finish their dinners?"

"I will," McTee said. Lily tugged at his sleeve, whispered in his ear when he leaned over. The lawyer turned to the lawmen and added, "My client suggests that we wait for the gentleman from the Bureau of Indian Affairs, so I need not repeat myself."

SAC Melvin's face turned red. The jump he'd gotten on Tall Wolf would soon be gone.

Worse, it would be clear he was the one who'd betrayed their working relationship.

"You know how soon he'll be here?" Melvin asked.

Annie nodded to the door. The lawyer and the cops saw a tall man wearing sunglasses enter the restaurant. Half the people in the restaurant were looking at him. Like the guy was a damn celebrity or something. He even had his own uniformed Mountie with him. A woman not much shorter than him in a sergeant's uniform. Damn nice looking, too.

Fucking Indian, Melvin thought.

Tracked him down like he'd left a trail of breadcrumbs.

CHAPTER 36

J ohn had followed a trail of logic. He figured Melvin, in the end, would be unable to resist screwing with him. He was Melvin's competitor, so he had it coming. But the SAC would make sure any case he brought to a U.S. attorney would be airtight. So, working in a foreign country, Melvin would be certain to have local law enforcement on hand. He would be able to show he had played strictly by the book when he brought Annie Forger and Lily White Bird home in handcuffs.

That being the case, Sergeant Bramley, at John's request, called ahead and asked if SAC Melvin had arrived yet. He found out that Melvin had gotten to Banff first. Two Mounties from Banff had been detailed to assist Melvin and a Superintendent Kent, who had jetted in from Ottawa. The local constables had last reported their position at a restaurant on Caribou Street.

It was the name of the restaurant that brought John up short.

The place was called Coyotes.

All the way up in Canada, what were the odds?

He wondered if Marlene Flower Moon was somehow behind all this.

He pushed through the front door.

Learning that Superintendent Kent had put the cops from both sides of the border in a holding pattern, John decided to spring for drinks for everyone. Even Melvin. A sign to the FBI man that any settling of accounts should take place south of the border.

John could justify the expense as the cost of making the

FBI look bad for failing to think of the gesture first. He was sure Marlene would never argue with that. If she did, he would never let her hear the end of it.

The Canadians were well pleased by John's solicitude.

Melvin gave him the stink eye.

The three uniformed Mounties ordered soft drinks. Kent and Melvin each had a scotch. John ordered spring water. He tipped twenty-five percent as a jab at Marlene. The two Banff constables stationed themselves near the front door where they could make sure the persons of interest did not attempt a surreptitious exit. Melvin and Kent drifted off to the far corner of the bar where they whispered to each other over their drinks.

Sergeant Bramley clinked her glass against John's

"Cheers," she said.

"*A votre santé.*" Health. They sipped their drinks.

Bramley asked, "Are you always such a sport or is there a purpose behind your generosity?"

John said, "You want me to give away all my secrets?"

He had a natural reserve. Wondering if a supernatural agency was pursuing a vendetta against you also inspired caution. But he had to guard against paranoia, too. If Sergeant Bramley was Coyote, he might be undone.

She said, "Not *all* of them. Not right away. Discovery is half the fun."

"You think we might meet again?"

"I take two weeks vacation in Florida every February and two weeks hiking and fishing in our provinces every August."

John asked, "Is that an invitation?"

"It is. In Florida, I like to wear high heels every so often, go dancing and not look down at the top of my partner's head."

"How do you know I dance?" John said.

"In the car, I saw you tapping your foot to the music. You've got rhythm."

Before the conversation could go further, McTee joined them.

"Thank you for your patience," he said. "We've finished our

meals and to the extent possible I'll answer your questions on behalf of my clients. My office is nearby. It's private and it's large enough to accommodate all of us."

"Fine by me," John said. "Let me see if —"

He stopped talking when he saw that one of the constables at the restaurant door was having a conversation by way of a portable radio. John couldn't overhear what was being said, but from the look on the cop's face it was serious. Bramley saw him, too, and was on her way over there.

McTee turned and he also saw something new was in the offing.

John told him, "Please ask your clients to give us a minute."

The lawyer's expression revealed that now he was eager to get his clients away from all the cops, but running out of the restaurant wouldn't look good. Might not even be possible.

McTee told John, "We'll order dessert."

The two local constables stayed inside the restaurant to keep an eye on Annie, Lily and McTee. The lawyer could leave if he wished. The sisters had to stay. John, Bramley, Melvin and Kent huddled with a local RCMP sergeant named Finnegan. The five of them had moved just up the street from Coyotes' entrance.

Finnegan told the others, "A couple of tourists found a body."

"Were the tourists Canadian?" Kent asked.

"Yes. Both from the Center of the Universe."

John and Melvin gave Finnegan a look.

Superintendent Kent clarified. "Toronto. People there can be a bit self-centered."

"A bit?" Bramley asked. She and Finnegan had to repress a laugh.

"Please continue with your report, Sergeant," Kent said.

"The tourists, their surname is Park, both had their mobile phones with them, but there was no signal where they found the body. They had to hike for over two hours before they could make a call. We sent a car as soon as we heard from them. It was nearly dark by then and too late to send a recovery party out. We'll do so at first light."

"Did the Parks touch the body?" Kent asked.

"They said they didn't. They were conflicted about that. They watch enough television to know a person shouldn't disturb a crime scene, if this is a crime scene, but they were also concerned some carnivore might happen by and have a snack. They —"

"What kind of carnivores are you talking about?" Melvin asked.

Finnegan said, "There are quite a few. Black bears, grizzlies, mountain lions, wolves and —"

"Coyotes," John said.

There was no getting away from it. Melvin looked like he'd be more comfortable with two-legged urban predators, too.

"Exactly," Finnegan said. "What the Parks did was cover the body with their two plastic rain ponchos and pin them down with rocks."

"Is that enough to keep animals away?" Melvin asked.

Finnegan shook his head. "Ordinarily, no. But the Parks are of Korean descent and they spread some kimchi in a ring around the body."

Bramley nodded. "That might work."

John asked, "Did the Parks take any pictures, so SAC Melvin and I might see whether we have a professional interest here?"

Finnegan said, "They took several photos, using their phones. Snapped them with the idea that if an animal did come along and wasn't deterred by a bit of garlic we'd have something to help with identification."

Melvin asked, "Did you print any of the photos?"

"We did," Finnegan said. "I have them in my car." He stepped over to a nearby Crown Victoria and came back with a three-ring binder. He handed it to Kent. Melvin moved in close for a look as the superintendent leafed through the photos.

John waited patiently.

Bramley liked that.

Much cooler than peering over a shoulder.

Kent passed the binder to John. He held it so Bramley could also see. After they'd glanced at all the shots, John went back to the third photo in the binder. It was shot almost straight down, looking at the face of the dead man. The back of the skull had been flattened, but the face was unmarked and the features were not displaced.

From a pocket, John took the picture of Randy Bear Heart and Lily White Bird posing as Bonnie and Clyde. He laid it on the facing page of the binder for comparison.

Rebecca Bramley said, "Well, well, well."

John handed the binder back to Kent. Melvin leaned in from one side, Finnegan from the other. All three heads bobbed. There was no question who the dead man was.

John said to Finnegan, "Was there any evidence Randy Bear Heart died before he fell? I didn't see any wounds on the body."

"Be right back," Finnegan said.

He went to his car again and returned with a clear plastic bag. In it there was a shell casing.

Finnegan said, "There were no obvious wounds, the Parks said, but they found a few of these not far from the body. They thought it would be okay to pick one up with a pen and put it in the sandwich bag, in case it rained or the wind scattered the others."

All five cops smiled.

Melvin said, "These people deserve some kind of commendation."

John asked, "Did you determine what kind of gun the casing came from?"

"We did. It's a .45 ACP cartridge, designed for the Colt semi-automatic pistol, the standard sidearm of the U.S. Army until they switched over to the Beretta."

"Christ," Melvin said, "there have to be millions of those things around. I've got one."

The three Canadian cops looked at the FBI man with critical eyes.

Melvin held his hands up. "Hey. It wasn't me. If I'd shot at him, I'd have hit him."

John said, "It wasn't him. There's another famous weapon that uses the same round."

"What's that?" Bramley asked.

"The Thompson submachine gun."

Melvin, Kent and Finnegan went into Coyotes to speak with McTee, if not his clients. Bramley had put a discreet hand on John's arm, indicating he should stay outside with her. She waited until the door had closed behind the others before she spoke.

"I've seen a Tommy gun recently," she said. "I was doing some window shopping."

"Where?"

"A store right here in Banff. The really interesting thing? It fits perfectly with that picture of yours. The place has an exhibit of Bonnie and Clyde."

John beamed at her and made the connection. "Is the store called Go Native?"

Lily had said she was going to open another store in San Diego. Maybe that was just misdirection. The real location of the new store was Banff.

But Bramley told him, "No, this place is called Go Hollywood."

Smart women, Lily and Annie, John thought. Adapt to new surroundings.

"What's the process for getting a search warrant in Canada?" John asked.

"Similar to the U.S. is my guess," Bramley said. "You go to a judge and apply for one. You describe the grounds for believing the thing to be searched for exists, that it's at the place to be searched, that a crime had been committed, that the place to be searched is where the thing will be found, and the thing to be found has evidentiary value."

John grinned. "I've always liked a smart woman."

Bramley shook her head, "You won't get far with me if all you think I've got is a good mind."

"We'll talk about the other stuff later."

"How about we talk about this? How much evidentiary value does the Tommy gun have if it turns out Mr. Bear Heart's body, in fact, has no bullet holes in it?"

John paused to think and said, "We'll have to make some other connections then, but imagine one of those carnival shooting gallery games. You have those up here?"

"Sure. You mean where the little metal guy scoots back and forth, changing direction when you score a hit?"

"That's the one. Now, imagine Randy Bear Heart as the little metal guy and Lily letting off bursts with the Tommy gun. You think she could run him off a cliff?"

Bramley said, "Damn, that'd be cold."

"Yeah. So how quick do you think you can get a search warrant for Go Hollywood?"

"I know a judge; he's a fishing buddy of my dad's."

"Always good to have friends," John said.

Bramley went to get the warrant. John went back into Coyotes.

He was still uneasy about that name.

The Trickster had to be somewhere nearby.

CHAPTER 37

Austin, Texas — July 17, the present

Detective Darton Blake could not believe how much paper-work was involved in impounding cash surrendered by a citizen, even one who was a) not the subject of a current investigation; b) not convicted of a felony; c) not a known associate of a convicted felon; d) not a party to pending civil litigation; e) not related by blood or marriage to the sworn officer or civilian employee to whom the money had been surrendered.

The same straining-at-gnats mentality pervaded the entire process. Darton had to provide the name of the person surrendering the money, the person's address and phone number, gender, DOB, physical appearance (photo preferred), make of car, state and number of license plates ... on and on.

A photographer and two detectives from the financial crimes unit had to be brought into the effort. The photographer shot a picture of the Central Market bag with the money in it, a picture of the bag empty, a picture of the cash stacked on a table. The detectives from financial crimes first had to determine that the money wasn't counterfeit. It wasn't, thank God, or the Secret Service would have had to be called. They had to determine if the money had been stolen from a federally chartered bank or credit union. It hadn't or the FBI would have had to be called.

Finally, they had to do a bill by bill count. The cops were not about to take Coy Wilson's word as to the total.

All of that was recorded on video with the shift commander

and Darton watching to make sure nobody stuffed any cash into his pocket. The official count coincided with Ms. Wilson's: one hundred thousand dollars, exactly. The money was placed in a plastic bin, sealed and stored in the department's locked evidence room.

Darton was told by his boss, homicide unit commander Lieutenant Ernie Calderon, to take the Central Market bag back to Ms. Wilson and get her signature in the six places required by the department regulations.

"You think this woman's playing straight with us, Darton?" the lieutenant asked.

"Yes, sir. She's hoping to get the money but she's protecting herself, too."

"Smart. But if she's honest, why didn't she stick around?"

"She's a musician."

Calderon smiled and nodded; that explained everything.

Artists were nowhere near normal people.

Darton drove out to Coy Wilson's house. She wasn't home. Lloyd Rucker, the next door neighbor, hadn't seen her that evening, he said. Nothing was ever easy. Darton folded the shopping bag neatly and put it into Coy's mail box along with one of his business cards asking her to call him.

By the time he got home, dinner was cold. His wife had to go out and show her mother how to download vacation pictures from her camera to her computer. Darton reheated his dinner, washed it down with two Lone Stars and played catch with his son, Amos, in the backyard until it got too dark to see the ball. He sent Amos off to his room with a hug and sat down in front of the television, looking for a baseball game to watch.

But he stopped his search to watch a cop show. Nobody did a bit of paperwork and the bad guys got caught in forty-three minutes flat — all the time you had when you took the commercials out of an hour-long show. Watching his fictional counterparts pursue justice reminded Darton that he'd wanted to call John Tall Wolf about Coy Wilson finding all that money. There was something else he wanted to bring up, too.

But he fell asleep on the sofa before he could remember what it was.

CHAPTER 38

Banff, Alberta — July 17, the present

John needed help from SAC Melvin, so he maintained a public spirit of sharing and told Melvin and Superintendent Kent that Sergeant Bramley had gone to secure a search warrant for the Go Hollywood store and what they hoped to find there.

Kent's eyes narrowed for a moment. It was clear that he thought Bramley should have checked with him first before seeking a warrant. Even so, he wasn't about to let the visiting Americans see a squabble between Mounties. John repressed a smile, thinking Bramley had shown no sign of worrying about putting the visiting poobah's nose out of joint.

He was getting to like her more all the time.

He'd have to brush up on his dance steps.

Melvin was skeptical about what he'd heard. He glanced at Annie Forger and Lily White Bird. They'd finished their dessert and were lingering over coffee. McTee was fidgeting, losing patience, and would soon start quoting Moses: *Let my people go.*

For the moment, though, Sergeant Finnegan and his two constables still provided a chilling effect.

"You really think these women would have the gall to hide an automatic weapon, one that might have been used in a homicide, right out in the open?" Melvin asked.

John shrugged. "Best I can say is maybe. Fits with the name of the store, though. It'd be a Hollywood type of trick to play — and we'd all look very foolish if we didn't check and it turned out to be what we're looking for."

Kent nodded, but had his own question. "Do we know, for a fact, that Ms. Forger and Ms. White are the leaseholders of the store?"

"Sergeant Bramley will find that out before she goes for the warrant." John hoped she would, as they hadn't discussed that little detail. Then to bolster his confidence, he said, "I'm willing to bet a month's pay that they are."

He looked at Melvin and Kent. Neither took his bet.

The FBI man asked his RCMP counterpart, "Can people up here own an automatic weapon?"

"No, not fully automatic firearms. Large capacity magazines are also prohibited."

"Break the law, go to jail?" Melvin asked.

"Yes."

John thought about that. He looked over at the two sisters. They met his gaze. They weren't smiling, but they might as well have been. Their expressions were smug, challenging. When McTee turned to see what was going on, John looked back at Melvin and Kent.

He asked the superintendent, "Do you have any laws against the possession of facsimile weapons?"

Kent said, "We do. Replica firearms meant to exactly or with near precision resemble the real thing are prohibited."

"Would a violator do time for that?" John asked.

"That would depend on the context. Using a replica in the commission of a crime, say, robbing a person or a business, would mean an added period of incarceration."

"What are you getting at, Tall Wolf?" Melvin asked.

"Just trying to get the lay of the land," John said deadpan. "It's a BIA thing."

Kent allowed himself a small smile. He was coming to like this new fellow.

The superintendent said, "Having the time to consider the matter, Mr. McTee over there is certain to say, even if we were to introduce a Thompson submachine gun into evidence, there's no way we could connect it to Mr. Bear Heart's death. He has no bullet holes in him, as far as we know. The cartridge the Parks retrieved has no time stamp on it. There's no way to show it's contemporaneous with the man's death. We can't show that one has anything to do with the other."

"What do you think about that?" John asked SAC Melvin.

Melvin thought the same thing John did: Kent needed to take his corset off.

If you couldn't fake the bad guys out of their socks, you shouldn't have a badge.

In the interest of maintaining a hands-across-the-border friendship, Melvin didn't share his opinion. He'd figured out by now the only reason Tall Wolf had been so forthcoming was that he needed something and couldn't get it by himself.

"I think," Melvin said, "as long as you don't lose sight of the law, it's not a bad thing to get creative."

"What do you mean?" Kent asked.

Melvin said, "Special Agent Tall Wolf is about to make a request — of each of us, I'm sure. What is it you need, Special Agent?"

"A working order Tommy gun. The FBI must have one somewhere. Quick delivery and permission to bring it here."

Melvin and Kent looked at each other.

The SAC was already on board; the superintendent was brought along.

All without a word being said.

Bureaucratic telepathy. *We claim the credit or the Indian gets the blame.*

"Tell us what you have in mind," Melvin told John.

He did.

Kent said, "That's positively diabolical."

The devil being the Western equivalent of the Trickster.

***

John, Sergeant Bramley, Constable Duncan Hargrove and his dog, Trudeau, stood at the front door of Go Hollywood. Bramley had obtained the keys to every lock on the premises from the landlord, the town council. Because the town of Banff was located in a national park, there was no freehold land, no private property. The town paid to lease the land on which it sat. Commercial growth was strictly limited. Businesses in Banff were in no position to quibble about the terms of their leases. When the search warrant for Go Hollywood was issued, the keys were forthcoming.

Not that Lily and Annie were aware at the moment that their store was being searched. They and their lawyer, Colin McTee, were listening to the questions SAC Melvin and Superintendent Kent had for them. Doubtlessly, McTee was refusing to let his clients answer any questions, but the sisters would still come to understand that law enforcement agencies in two countries considered them persons of interest in a number of felonies.

It was possible Lily and Annie thought they had outsmarted anyone who might seek to arrest, try and imprison them, but they might be uneasy wondering where John was, why he wasn't with the other cops questioning them, and what he might be up to elsewhere.

If so, so much the better. Even experienced criminals made mistakes when they got nervous.

Bramley told John, "We're in. Let's see what we've got here."

Trudeau, a sleek black Lab trained in bomb detection for the RCMP at Lackland Air Force Base in San Antonio, Texas, awaited her command. The dog was shivering in anticipation.

Constable Hargrove told her, "*Vas-y.*"

Go. Tail wagging the dog raced into the store.

Sergeant Bramley, exhibiting just what a fine mind she had, had written the search warrant request not only for a Thompson submachine gun but also for any container in which such a weapon might be concealed or carried.

She had explained her reasoning to John.

"These women had to surprise this Bear Heart guy with

their big, bad gun, right? They surely didn't march him up the mountainside with the weapon in plain sight. So I thought we better look for a knapsack or something."

John had smiled at her. Having heard Bramley's idea he'd been inspired.

"Can you get us a dog? You shoot off an automatic weapon and stick it inside some sort of carrying case, there have to be fumes trapped inside it."

The sisters might have stored or ditched the Tommy gun somewhere else, but it never hurt to build up whatever incriminating evidence you could.

Trudeau made a bee line to the back room of the store. Following behind the others, John glanced at the display case positioned at the rear of the show room. In it he saw two sets of clothes: hats, shoes, a man's suit, a blouse and a skirt. A card read: *Original wardrobe items from the film "Bonnie and Clyde," starring Warren Beatty and Faye Dunaway.*

Between the two period costumes was a Tommy gun. Close up, it was easy to see it was fake. There was another card in the case next to the gun, but Trudeau started to bark and John was eager to see what the dog had found.

Trudeau, vibrating with excitement, sat in front of a large wicker picnic hamper resting on a table. The top of the hamper was open and even the humans in the room could detect the scent of cordite. John looked up and saw an open skylight. The hamper was being aired out. One or both of the sisters hadn't wanted to part with it. Hargrove stroked Trudeau's head.

He said, "*Bonne fille.*" Good girl. "*Il y a quelque chose d'autre?*" Anything else.

The lab yipped and moved to a corner of the room. Hanging from hooks on the wall above the dog were two blond wigs. John and Bramley moved in to sniff. More cordite.

"*C'est tout?*" Hargrove asked. Trudeau stayed put. The dog handler turned to Bramley. "That's all, Sergeant."

"Thank you, Constable," she said. "Trudeau is a credit to the force."

Hargrove beamed. "Yes, ma'am." He and the dog left.

Bramley looked at John. "So what do you think, Special Agent? Anything here that helps the cause?"

John nodded. "I've already got Lily."

"You do?"

"Yes." He told her how, and asked that she keep it to herself. "Now, I have an idea that might help us nab Annie, too." Swearing Bramley to secrecy, he shared that, too.

The RCMP sergeant smiled like a kid with an ice cream cone.

She thought she might be falling in love.

Before John and Bramley left the store with the wicker hamper, they stopped to read the other card in the display case: *Every item in this store is guaranteed authentic, except the Thompson submachine gun. It's a toy.*

Bramley had a key to the case and she opened it. The gun was plastic. It had been locked away from the public and the card describing it as a toy eliminated any possible charge of intent to deceive. It would be of no use in any criminal prosecution.

That wouldn't stymie John's plan in the least.

Nor did it keep John from wondering how Lily and Annie had come by signature costume pieces from a classic movie.

CHAPTER 39

Austin, Texas — July 18, the present

D arton Blake awoke in his darkened living room. He'd thought
he'd left a light on; he knew he'd left the TV on. Both had been
turned off. A pillow had been tucked under his head and a blanket
was draped over him. There was a hint of perfume on the pillow.
Jacy had come home and taken pity on a hardworking cop. The
scent of the Saint Laurent Opium was her signal that a good time
was available.

He glanced at his watch. One-ten. Not too late, he hoped. They
could have their time together and get a reasonable amount of
sleep before the alarm went off. He swung his feet off the sofa —
and the moment they hit the floor he remembered he should call
John Tall Wolf about the money Coy Wilson had found in the safe
deposit box.

One-eleven now. Would Tall Wolf be asleep? Would he mind
being disturbed to hear the news? Would Darton even remember
to call him if he waited until later? He decided to take a chance.
Better the BIA agent should lose a little sleep than receive the
information too late. He tapped John's number into his phone.

"Hello."

"Shit, I did wake you," Darton said. "I'm sorry."

John said, "Just dozing. Still thinking about things."

"I won't ask about what right now. Just want to give you a
heads-up on some news."

Darton told John about Coy's discovery of the money.

John told Darton about the situation in Banff.

"Coy found the money in a bank box?" he asked. "And she found the key just yesterday in Jackson's guitar case?"

"That's right," Darton said.

"Leaving his guitar behind must mean Jackson had expected to come home."

"Yeah, it does."

"That suggest anything to you?" John asked.

"If you're saying his mom set him up, that'd be awful damn cold."

"Maybe Randy was just giving Lily a hard time, getting a little physical. She called her son to settle him down, but things got out of hand."

Darton said, "Could be. It's bad enough when cops referee a domestic fight. Anybody else does it, he's really asking for trouble. So you think there's payback after all this time? These two women killed the boyfriend they shared?"

"Payback might be part of their rationale, something to tell themselves. Mostly, though, what could they have said if they'd been caught with Randy? They'd be his accomplices."

John told Darton what he had in mind for the two sisters.

"That's great," Darton said. "Wish I could be there. You should see how big I'm smiling right now. Hey, before I forget, this might be useful to your plan. After Coy dropped all that money on me and drove off, I thought I should have asked her, did she find anything else in that lock box?"

John said, "Yeah, that'd be good to know." And he thought of how he might improve his plan. "Call Ms. Wilson first thing in the morning. See how she'd feel about making a quick trip to Banff."

CHAPTER 40

Banff, Alberta — July 18, the present

John decided to take the same risk Darton had taken minutes earlier.

He called Boston and woke Guy Forger.

"Sorry to disturb you. This is Special Agent Tall Wolf."

"Damn, man. Couldn't it have waited 'til morning?"

"Half could, half couldn't. Can you tell me whose name is on the deed to the house where you live?"

"Yeah, shit, I know that. Pyewacket Holdings. Sounds Native American, but it isn't."

John said, "It was the name of a cat, a familiar, belonging to a witch."

Guy grunted. "That's pretty good. You must've paid attention in school. Is that it?"

"One more thing," John said. "How about you and Louie meet me in Banff later today?"

John made one more call. Maurice Satterly had been asleep, too.

"Sorry to disturb you, sir," John said, "but this might help me find out what happened to Vern Forger."

"If that's the case," Satterly said, "you can talk 'til dawn. I won't get any sleep now."

"I assume Vern Forger had an agent who negotiated his contracts with you."

"Of course."

"May I have his name and his phone number, if you have it handy?"

The Vancouver GM gave John the information from memory. Harvey Kingsbury and a phone number in Toronto.

"How will that help you?" Satterly asked.

"Might be leverage. Might help me run a bluff. Would you know how Annie Forger got along with Mr. Kingsbury?"

Satterly laughed. "Harvey skinned us pretty good on Vern's last contract. There were two pictures on the sports page of the *Vancouver Sun* to mark that occasion. In one Mrs. Forger was kissing Vern; in the other she was kissing Harvey."

John might have gotten away disturbing one man's sleep, but having pulled a second sleeper from his pillow, karma was due and paid. Marlene Flower Moon banged on the door to John's hotel room a half-hour before his alarm would have roused him. The conversations he'd had with Darton Blake, Guy Forger and Maurice Satterly had left him feeling confident that he'd be able to get both Lily and Annie into court.

Marlene hammered the door again.

"I know you're in there, Tall Wolf. I can hear you breathing."

My, what big ears you have, Coyote, John thought.

"I'm here," he said, getting out of bed. "I'm going to clean up. I'll meet you in the hotel restaurant. Don't order anything for me."

"You won't let me in?"

John laughed. If she could hear him breathe, she could hear that, too.

When John joined Marlene for breakfast, the only thing waiting on the table for him was a glass of water.

Nodding at the glass, Marlene said, "I'm told that comes from a nearby stream, and it was brought at the restaurant's initiative not my request."

A waitress came to the table and John asked for a glass of

orange juice.

He declined her offer of coffee.

After she left, Marlene asked, "No caffeine for you? No stimulants at all?"

"I find life exciting enough. What are you doing here?"

"I received a call from Mr. McTee on behalf of his clients."

"You want to be in on the arrest?" John asked.

"Mr. McTee led me to believe there are no grounds for an arrest. That being the case, I was wondering what you're doing here."

John sat back and looked at his boss. She'd been dogging his heels the whole way through this case. He couldn't help but think she had a personal stake in its outcome.

He asked her, "You hear about Randy Bear Heart going cliff-diving without an ocean anywhere in sight?"

Marlene shrugged. "A multiple murderer and bank robber comes to a bad end, who's going to shed a tear?"

John was tempted to ask if there was *anything* that might make Marlene weep, but he went in a different direction.

"Did Mr. McTee tell you I visited the shop Lily White Bird and Annie Forger operate in town? It's called Go Hollywood. They have this show case display of two outfits from the movie 'Bonnie and Clyde.'"

"No, he didn't tell me that."

"Maybe I forgot to tell him."

Marlene's eyes narrowed. John thought he saw a yellow light through the slitted lids.

"I hope you didn't forget to obtain a search warrant," she said.

"A colleague with the RCMP did that. After I came back to my room, I did a computer search. There are businesses in Los Angeles that sell props and wardrobe items from various movies. From what I could learn, the pieces in Go Hollywood would have cost tens of thousands of dollars, minimum. I wouldn't be surprised if their value is much higher."

Marlene had a cup of coffee in front of her. She opened her

mouth to take a sip, revealing what John had long thought to be the four sharpest canine teeth he'd ever seen in a human mouth.

"What's your point?" she asked.

"Well, there are a few. For instance, why would Randy Bear Heart have stolen sacred relics from Mercy Ridge in the first place? The obvious answer is for the money he could gain by selling them, but I don't think that was it. I think Randy saw the items he stole as an insurance policy. If the tribe didn't give the white cops any help in finding him, he'd have somebody send them back after he was past caring."

"I told you nothing was stolen," Marlene said.

"Yes, you did, but Annie Forger told me the opposite. Of course, if she'd already returned the stolen goods, I could look for them for the rest of my life without finding them. So letting me know about the theft, that could have been a useful diversion."

"If you're right about that, you'll never know who told you the truth, me or Ms. Forger."

The waitress brought John's orange juice. He took a sip and told her he wouldn't need anything else.

When the two of them were alone again, John said, "Lily and Annie were both obsessed by Randy Bear Heart, but there's no compulsion as strong as self-preservation. Not to get dragged down by Randy when *his* obsessions finally did him in. They must have planned for at least the possibility of doing him in long before they acted. Fact is, they'd be better off without him. That's not to say the relics he stole didn't have any value. They might be swapped for, say, Hollywood memorabilia. That would have been far more satisfying than just giving them back."

"How could you ever prove that?" Marlene asked.

John said, "It probably wouldn't be too hard. All I have to do is find out who owned the costumes on display at Go Hollywood before Lily and Annie came to possess them. Once I know who that is, I'll bet I can find out who bought them. Maybe someone at or connected to Mercy Ridge. Someone who might have wanted to keep Lily and Annie happy."

Marlene grimaced, bringing her canines back into view.

This time, she added a low growl.

Instead of drawing back, John leaned forward. The wolf did not fear the coyote.

"This isn't a priority for me as long as I get to take Lily and Annie down. If you try to thwart me on that, I'll have a talk with SAC Melvin, let him decide how to handle things. He might even look into the war chest you're building for your eventual political ambitions. If Lily and Annie were helping the cause, you want to send that money back fast. Otherwise, it might look like they were trying to bribe a federal official, and you were aiding accomplices to several felonies."

With Marlene on their side, if she was, it would be no wonder the two sisters thought they were off the hook. John was sure they would be outraged when Marlene didn't come through for them. But what could they say, their payoff hadn't been honored?

Maybe they would.

Maybe John would need a new job soon.

The waitress returned and asked if they'd like anything else.

Marlene stood and told John, "You're so generous with your expense account these days, you can pick up the check."

So she'd found out he'd bought a round of drinks.

It was a small enough victory to allow her.

He paid the tab in cash.

CHAPTER 41

Banff, Alberta — July 18, the present

Superintendent Manley Kent had invoked the hoariest of law enforcement clichés without blushing. He'd told Lily White Bird and Annie Forger not to leave town. As Banff covered an area of less than four square kilometers, watching the sisters would not require a great deal of manpower. Lily and Annie had been warned of the consequences of violating Kent's order. They would lose the right to operate their business in Banff and Annie's permanent resident status would be jeopardized. They would also be taken into custody under a material witness warrant until the investigation was concluded.

Colin McTee said he would fight the warrant, but the sisters held him back. They wanted to be seen as innocents with nothing to fear or hide. As far as they knew, John Tall Wolf was still the only real threat against them and Marlene Flower Moon still had their backs.

John stepped out of the hotel and took a look around. You liked beautiful mountain vistas in sparkling sunlight, Banff would be a tough place to beat. As long as no one firing a Tommy gun herded you off a cliff.

Pretty damn slick way for two girls from Mercy Ridge to get rid of a man who'd lost their favor. Too bad for them they didn't think things through just a step or two further. They might have gotten away with it all.

No, not really. Not if the spirit of Daniel Red Hawk had anything to say about it.

John walked through town, asking himself if he was overlooking anything. As if in reply, his ring-tone sounded. Darton Blake was calling from Austin with good news.

"Coy Wilson is on her way up to Canada. Pulled some strings to get her the quickest connections."

John said, "That's great. Thanks."

"It gets even better."

"How's that?"

"There was something else in that lock box," Darton said. "A confession."

When John heard the details, he knew why Daniel Red Hawk's cloud had been smiling.

CHAPTER 42

Calgary, Alberta — July 18, the present

John and Sergeant Bramley met Coy Wilson at Calgary International Airport. The musician had made the trip with her guitar. She'd also brought a small carryon bag and an air of anxiety. She shook hands with John, and then Bramley stepped forward.

"I've seen you perform," she said, shaking Coy's hand. "You've played the Stampede at the Saddledome, right?"

"I have," Coy said, her jitters easing a bit.

Bramley turned to John. "This woman is proof positive that playing lead guitar isn't just for guys. She knocks me out."

John said, "I'll hit iTunes the first chance I get."

Coy eyed him. "She's not BS-ing me. I don't know about you."

John said, "Rock, pop, country, gospel: I like it all."

"*I* got him to consider country, and he's not so big on metal."

Coy smiled and looked at the two of them. "You're not doing good cop, bad cop, are you?"

John and Bramley laughed. It was plain Ms. Wilson had never seen the real thing.

"She thinks we don't appreciate culture," Bramley told John.

They found a booth at the Kelsey's restaurant in the airport and ordered soft drinks. Bramley, in uniform, took the outside seat next to John to keep their space clear of idlers. Coy sat opposite them. John leaned forward.

With a straight face, he said, "You'll notice we made sure

there's no one blocking your exit in case you feel the urge to run."

"Men," Bramley said, shaking her head. "Thank you for coming on such short notice, Ms. Wilson. I'll remind Special Agent Tall Wolf to watch his manners as necessary."

They were teasing her now, Coy knew, but it was helping.

She started to relax. Smiled at them.

"Detective Blake told me it was important for me to come."

John said, "He's a good guy. May I see the letter you found in your safe deposit box?"

Coy took a black leather folio out of her bag. She flipped it open, revealing a pad of lined paper. On the top page, handwritten in blue ink, were two four-line blocks of writing. Trained observers, both John and Bramley noticed. Coy saw them looking.

"A song I started to write on the flight up here," she told them.

"You feeling good about what you have so far?" Bramley asked.

Coy grinned. "Now, you sound like a producer, but yeah, I am."

"Hope I get to hear it someday."

Coy knew she was being flattered, but the kind words were having the desired effect.

The two cops were making her feel safe instead of threatened.

"Here's what you want," she told John. She took out a sheet of unlined paper from the back of the notepad and handed it to him.

He read the message twice, handed it to Bramley.

"That should do it, right?" Coy asked. "A signed confession is as good as it gets, isn't it?"

The second question drew Bramley's attention as she finished reading.

"Detective Blake kept the original?" John asked.

Coy nodded.

"He made the copy for you to give to me?"

"Yes."

"Did you notice the top edge of the photocopy, Sergeant Bramley?"

"I did," she said.

"What about it?" Coy asked.

Bramley handed the piece of paper to her and said, "The page that was copied has perforations across the top."

Coy bobbed her head. "I saw that, but so what?"

"It suggests the confession you found in that lock box was torn off a pad of paper, and maybe the pad belonged to Ms. White. A defense attorney might say Jackson stole it from his mother."

"I didn't steal it," Coy said. "My name was on that lock box account, and I gave it to the police. So they came by it honestly, too."

"That might be enough for a reasonable judge," John said. "But if you get one of those legal sticklers, he might agree with the argument that if the confession was stolen in the first place, it doesn't matter if anyone came by it honestly after that."

"Well, hell, what do we do now?" Coy asked.

John said in a calm tone, "You could go home right now and have a clear conscience."

"But you've got something else in mind. Detective Blake told me that, but he wouldn't say what it was."

"I do have something in mind," John said. "Do you want to hear what it is?"

Coy thought about it for a minute.

"Will your plan help me feel better about what happened to Jackson?"

"I'll tell you and you can decide."

Coy heard John out and nodded.

"I can do that," she said. "I *want* to do it."

John smiled. Now, all they had to do was wait for Guy and Louie to arrive.

While they waited for the Forger brothers, Sergeant Bramley got Superintendent Kent's mobile phone number for John. He left Bramley and Coy Wilson chatting about music in the restaurant, found a seat in a quiet stretch of the concourse and called Kent.

"This might sound a bit odd, Superintendent," John said, "but please bear with me. How do you feel about sports agents?"

"Greedy bastards, the lot of them," Kent said, playing along. "They turn athletes into mercenaries and sports fans into fools."

"Are you familiar with the name Harvey Kingsbury?"

"He's the worst of the worst, at least as far as professional hockey is concerned."

John smiled. He was counting on Kent being typically Canadian in his passion for the sport.

"How would you like to have a chance to rattle his cage?"

Kent's evil chuckle would have done credit to Darth Vader.

"I started liking you, Special Agent Tall Wolf, when you bought drinks for the sergeant and the constables, not just SAC Melvin and me. If, within the context of our case, you can give me reason to have a go at Harvey Kingsbury, I'd be obliged to buy you a drink."

"I'm a cheap date, Superintendent. Mostly, I drink water. But here's what I have in mind."

Kent listened without interruption and then said, "That's not only a legitimate idea, it might be the proverbial final nail in the coffin."

"We can hope," John said.

"I'll get right on it," Kent told him.

CHAPTER 43

Banff, Alberta — July 18, the present

Annie Forger and Lily White Bird sat looking out the living room windows of the single family home they rented on Muskrat Street. The house was a modern take on a two-story log cabin. There were three bedrooms, two baths, extensive landscaping and heart-stopping mountain views.

The cash flow from Go Hollywood met their living expenses in town and provided a small surplus. The arrangement allowed each sister to remain well heeled and to carefully tend her investments and watch her money grow. It was an immensely gratifying situation for two girls who had grown up poor at Mercy Ridge.

The simple fact that they were allowed to live in Banff showed how far they'd come. You couldn't just move to town at whim, write a fat check and buy a house. You had to demonstrate "a need to reside" in Banff to be allowed to live there. Residential land was available only for community use. People who simply wanted to buy a recreational or second home were out of luck.

Banff was a small jewel and its planning commission meant to keep it that way.

Snubbing the rich might have seemed an odd strategy for a resort destination, but the monied classes preferred to come and go anyway. When they appeared, they were treated lavishly and urged to return. They just couldn't put down roots.

Annie and Lily, on the other hand, felt the natural beauty was so compelling they wanted to call Banff home. They joked with each other that the town was what a reservation in heaven must look like, and the fact that they'd been admitted was no mean feat.

They had met one of the requirements for showing a need to reside: They operated a business in town, and Go Hollywood employed three people other than themselves. Annie had been the first to visit Banff on a ski trip with her late husband, Vern. After his death, she'd brought Lily to see it. If anything, Lily loved the town even more than Annie. She'd been the one who had investigated what it would take to live there. She was the one who first expressed to the local officials an interest in opening a business there and cited her success in running Go Native in Austin as a credential to make a go of it in Banff.

Jackson was dead by the time they'd realized their plan, and when Guy and Louie made an occasional visit they were put up in a hotel. That had left only one person to consider: Randy.

He'd been the one who had inspired both of them to get out of Mercy Ridge.

Lily looked at her sister and asked, "How are you feeling?"

"Relieved. Maybe a bit sad."

Annie knew Lily was asking her about Randy being dead.

"How about you?" Annie asked.

"The same, and a little scared, too."

"About Tall Wolf?"

"Him, too. Where the hell did that guy come from?"

"He works for Marlene," Annie said.

"Yeah, well, she should keep him the hell away from us."

"She's trying. My feeling was, Tall Wolf was only supposed to report to Marlene what the FBI was doing."

Lily shook her head. "We think we're so much smarter than men, even someone like Randy, but they still seem to get their way most of the time."

"What else scares you?" Annie asked. "You said, 'him, too,' about Tall Wolf."

"I'm more scared about what we're becoming, you and me."

Annie said, "It's more than becoming; it's what we already are.

Randy was just the latest for both of us. If it makes you feel any better I have twice as much blood on my hands as you."

"You haven't lost a son," Lily said.

"No, I've just abandoned two of them."

"It seems like everything's coming apart," Lily said.

Annie nodded. "I sure as hell wish I had closed up my house in Rapid City a week earlier. Wish I hadn't been so curious I had to go get a look at Tall Wolf. I didn't tell you, but I was half-tempted to have someone slip something into one of his drinks, the way I did with Vern."

"Why didn't you?" Lily asked. "Would you have felt guilty this time?"

Annie shook her head. "He told me his mother's a *curandera*. That scared me. Healers are supposed to be good people, but they make me nervous. They know too many secrets. Get one of them mad at you, who knows what she might do?"

"Jesus," Lily said.

Annie saw her sister was looking out the window again.

Guy and Louie and a blonde-haired woman were coming up their walk.

"Who's the woman?" Annie asked.

"Coy Wilson. Jackson's old girlfriend."

The sisters looked at each other, wondering the same thing.

What was going on here?

A block up Muskrat Street, John sat with SAC Melvin and Superintendent Kent in an Itasca Reyo. With them were Sergeant Bramley and another Mountie, both in plain clothes. The motorhome was parked in the driveway of a cooperating resident. A moment earlier, the five cops had heard Coy, Guy and Louie do a final check of the body mikes they wore.

Coy and Guy had gone with the standard, "Testing. One, two, three."

Louie had ad libbed. "Hey, Mom gets locked up, who gives me my allowance?"

Melvin and Kent exchanged a look of concern.

John said, "He's just messing with us."

He hoped so, anyway. They were working off his plan. The three young people were going to do the heavy lifting, and then John would step in and wrap things up.

Melvin had wanted to do the star turn that brought the curtain down.

Kent overruled him. "This is Special Agent Tall Wolf's show. We'll let him carry it off."

Or not.

There was an element of risk. Everyone in the vehicle considered the sisters to be cunning killers. Whether their disregard for life would extend to their offspring and the de facto widow of a lost son was an open question. If things went wrong ...

Even Melvin could see Kent's point.

Let the Indian carry the weight.

Kent's offer to buy John a drink notwithstanding.

They heard a doorbell ring and a door open.

Lily exclaimed, "Coy!"

Annie cried out, "Guy, Louie!"

"Reception five by five," said the Mountie monitoring the audio recorder.

Perfect.

Kerry Colcroft was a high honors graduate of McGill Law. Her father, a senior partner at a Toronto law firm, had paid for his daughter's education and had guided her in a choice of careers from the time she had turned twelve.

"Family law, Daddy? Divorces?" Kerry had asked when told what her lot in life would be.

"People are forever choosing the wrong mates, my dear. You'll never lack for work."

Charles Colcroft also hoped that witnessing the messes people made of their lives would incline his only child to be judicious in choosing her own husband. In truth, he hoped she would allow him to arrange a marriage for her.

Kerry disappointed her father in many ways.

She went into criminal defense work, and she moved to the West to become Colin McTee's associate. She was still dealing with people who'd botched their lives, but there was drama, grit and excitement to the work far beyond the cliché of extramarital sex. If her father were still speaking to her, though, he might be pleased to learn that she had decided she would never take up with anyone who so much as fudged his tax returns.

Criminals invariably overestimated their own intelligence.

Mr. McTee on the other hand —

Three people walked up to the door of the house on Muskrat Street she'd been assigned to watch from the car she used to circle the block. The car Annie and Lily might have noticed had they not been so self-preoccupied.

Mr. McTee was smart enough to have her safeguard his clients.

Watch for the police or anyone else to approach them.

If that were to happen, he'd told her, she need do only one thing.

Call him at once.

Lily hugged Coy. She had always liked the girl, always loved the music she and Jackson had made together. They could have made it big time if they'd chosen any name for the band other than Red Hawk. The use of her late husband's name had worried Lily. Mentioning it to Randy and the public notice it might bring had led to their argument over how to handle the matter. The dispute had started the chain of events that led to Jackson's death.

Randy had told Lily that if Jackson didn't change the band's name maybe he'd cut off one or two of the boy's guitar-playing fingers. See how well he could play then. Or maybe he'd just tell Jackson it was dear old Mom who'd plugged Red Hawk.

Lily hadn't cared for either idea, but Randy said he had to do something because he sure as hell wasn't going to get locked up after all this time.

Annie loved her sons. She just had a problem looking at them. They both resembled their father, the likeness growing stronger as they got older. A sense of chill surprise struck Annie that it wouldn't be long before Guy and Louie reached the age at which Vern had died.

Her epiphany led to fear. Would her sons live longer than their father had? There was no reason to think they wouldn't. Unless they met someone like her. She had loved Vern; she just hadn't been able to forget Randy. When Vern was off on a road trip with the team, Annie made excuses to travel, too. She flew down to Las Vegas for weekends with Randy.

She didn't do it every time Vern traveled, but he thought she should stay home.

All the time. He was the one making the money, he said, and lots of it.

Annie loved the money, but not having it used as a threat against her. She'd never admitted to going off to see a man. It hadn't occurred to her in the early days that Vern might be fooling around on the road. Then the wife of a teammate told Annie that her husband had something serious going on with a woman in Toronto, and she better find a lawyer to protect her interests.

She went to Randy instead. Problem solved. Shame about Teddy and Bill, though.

She hadn't asked for that.

Looking at her sons now, she realized that Vern never would have abandoned them emotionally, the way she had. He might have found another wife, but he would have come on the run had his boys needed him. He would have taken care of her financially, as long as his divorce lawyer hadn't found out about Randy. Which he almost certainly would have.

She'd really had no choice.

Hell of a thing, the way life could work out.

The phone rang in the house on Muskrat Street.

Annie said, "I'll get it." Everyone in the room watched her say hello. She listened for a moment and said, "No, no. Everything's fine. My sons and a friend of Lily's, that's all."

She clicked off and gave Lily a nod.

Annie told her sister, "That was Colin's friend, Kerry. Seeing if everything's all right."

They both felt reassured their lawyer had someone watching out for the cops.

Lily was the one to ask the question, "Coy, do you and the boys know each other?"

"We met earlier today," Coy said.

Annie looked at her sons. "Where did you meet?"

Guy told her, "The airport in Calgary."

Louie's nod affirmed the point.

"But what was the reason for the three of you to get together?" Lily asked.

Both sisters were starting to feel uneasy. The lives they'd lived had sharp dividing lines. Having those boundaries disappear before their eyes carried with it a sense of menace.

"I called them," Coy said. "They agreed to fly out and meet me."

Annie asked with an edge to her voice, "Why did you want to meet with my sons?"

Coy shrugged. "Money, of course. You think maybe we could get something to drink?"

Guy said, "Yeah, and maybe we should all be sitting down for this little chat."

In the motorhome up the block, John said, "We're off to a good start. Coy sounds like a natural for this, and Guy's going to be strong, too."

"Yeah, but what about the younger brother, Louie?" Melvin asked. "He could still be the joker in the deck."

John nodded. "Could be, but I think he'll follow Guy's lead."

Kent looked at the two Americans. If things went wrong, he'd have to apportion the blame to both of them in order to escape most of it himself. He'd have been more nervous if SAC Melvin had been the one taking the lead. Of the two Yanks, he thought Tall Wolf was the smarter.

Now, they'd have to see if he was lucky as well.

Kent's mobile phone chirped and he answered by giving his name.

"Yes, I see," he said. "Of course. I'm sure you did your best."

John and Melvin looked at him as he broke the connection.

Kent said, "A bit of bad luck, I'm afraid. Harvey Kingsbury freely admitted a business relationship with Ms. Forger, but swears he did nothing illegal, and knows of nothing illegal any of his clients might have done."

John frowned. He'd been counting on Kingsbury to provide a documentary link between Annie Forger and Randy Bear Heart. Now —

"Under a bit of prodding, though," Kent continued, "Kingsbury did admit to providing Ms. Forger with one hundred thousand dollars cash on three separate occasions, three hundred thousand total. He said she repaid him on schedule."

Melvin asked, "U.S. dollars or Canadian?"

"U.S.," Kent said.

John wanted to know the dates Kingsbury provided the money.

Kent got back on the phone and came up with the information.

The first time Annie got the cash from Kingsbury was the week before Vern Forger and his teammates had died. Nobody in the van believed that was a coincidence. The question was how to prove the money paid for the killings.

"Get her to talk," John said.

He got up and grabbed the picnic hamper they'd seized from Go Hollywood.

Sergeant Bramley opened the door to the motorhome for John. She stepped out to let him exit. As he passed her, his body blocking the view of the others, she slipped him a small semi-auto, only seven rounds in the clip, but it was better than yelling for help should things get iffy.

Colin McTee sat at his desk, drumming his fingers on the polished teak.

He hated coincidences as much as any cop did. Annie Forger's sons and a friend of Lily's showing up together the day after the two sisters had been confronted by the RCMP, the FBI and the BIA just didn't wash. Someone was trying to be clever here.

That had to be the case even if Kerry had it right that there had been no alarm in his client's voice when they'd spoken. McTee had ordered his associate to stop orbiting the block and park directly across the street from the sisters' residence, telling Kerry to call him immediately if the cops showed up. That was a reasonable precaution. He was a busy man, but if he wasn't able to concentrate on anything else —

His phone rang. Kerry was calling back.

"A man is approaching the house," she said. "He's not in uniform."

"Please describe him."

Kerry did so.

Tall Wolf, no doubt in McTee's mind.

Would Superintendent Kent have allowed an American to go about armed in Canada?

He shouldn't have, but who knew how much influence these people had?

He was about to ask for his associate's opinion on the matter, as if she were equipped even to guess whether a man might be armed, when Kerry said, "He's carrying a picnic hamper."

McTee found that more ominous than if Tall Wolf had had a gun in hand.

What was an American federal agent doing with a picnic hamper?

What the hell did he have in there?

"I'll be right there, Ms. Colcroft. Do nothing unless our clients are led out of their house under arrest. If that's the case, do your best to stall the authorities until I arrive."

He'd hired the young woman for her pluck as well as her intelligence.

Now, McTee might see how good his judgment was.

At the airport in Calgary, the Forger brothers had met Coy Wilson and had been given the copy of Lily White Bird's confession to read. How Lily had shot and killed Daniel Red Hawk, and how Coy had taken a call from a distraught Lily on the night their cousin Jackson had disappeared. Lily had abruptly sold her store and left town soon after. Jackson's body had recently been found in chains in the dry bed of Lake Travis in Austin, his skull cleaved by a sharp object. However, it was unlikely that a woman acting alone would kill and dispose of her own son in such a manner. John Tall Wolf suspected Randy Bear Heart was the killer.

They'd also heard from John of his suspicion that someone working with or for Bear Heart had slipped a mickey to the guy who'd crashed the car in which their father had died.

The news that their mother had been involved in killing their father had hit the boys like a cross-check into the boards. Guy had thought Louie might bawl, but his kid brother sat there stone faced and nodding as if things made sense to him for the first time. Having had the opportunity to think about it, Guy had to agree.

You were the kind of woman who killed your husband, maybe you wouldn't be so hot to have his sons around either.

Annie and Lily were in the kitchen together now, getting drinks for their guests.

Guy lowered his head and whispered into his mike, "Don't see any guns so far."

Coy, Guy and Louie sat on one side of the dining room table. Lily and Annie took two chairs on the opposite side. They brought out bottles of spring water and glasses for their guests. A bowl of mixed nuts sat within everyone's reach.

Louie was the only one to fill his glass and take a sip of water.

Coy and Guy had the same thought: Throw the bottles at Lily and Annie, if need be.

"You've got two choices here," Coy told the sisters. "You can pay us or we can call the cops."

"What would you have to tell the police that would be worth any money?" Annie asked.

Louie took the copy of Lily's confession out of his pocket and said, "Aunt Lily killed her husband and is an accomplice to the murder of her own son."

It was John's idea to have Louie spring the surprise, throw the sisters off balance, not let them know from which direction the next blow might come.

When Lily looked at Coy she saw a stone mask.

Louie passed the confession to his mother. She saw it was a photostat and there would be no point ripping it to shreds. She read it and turned to her sister with a look of contempt.

"How could you be so stupid?" she asked Lily.

That was when John walked into the house, picnic hamper on one arm, and said, "Now, now, Ms. Forger. You weren't so smart yourself."

"He's in," the Mountie monitoring the recorder in the motorhome said.

"Alert all units to be ready to move," Kent told him, "but not until I give the word."

As the Mountie relayed his instructions, Kent leaned close to Melvin and whispered, "Tell me honestly, Gilbert, would you want to be in Tall Wolf's shoes right now?"

"Maybe. If I had a gun."

Bramley, who had very keen hearing, thought, *You wouldn't have gotten it from me, mister.*

"Where did you get that?" Annie demanded, looking at the

picnic hamper.

John took an empty chair, positioned it two feet from the head of the table. There was a good eight feet between him and Louie. The sisters would have to turn their heads to look from one to the other. Distractions would be available, should they become necessary.

"Found it in the back room of Go Hollywood," John said. "Courtesy of a search warrant obtained by the RCMP."

He took the Tommy gun out of the the hamper and placed it on his lap.

"You can't have that," Lily blurted. "We got rid of it."

"Shut up!" Annie ordered.

Coy said, "Didn't get rid of it good enough apparently."

"We threw it in the Bow Riv—"

A resounding slap from Annie cut Lily short.

"Be quiet!" she commanded.

Guy and Louie exchanged a look. They no longer had any doubt Mom could be dangerous.

A drop of blood appeared at the tip of Lily's nose. Coy handed her a handkerchief, a look of pity now on her face.

Lily dabbed at the blood and said, "Thank you."

Annie shook her head in disgust and told her sister. "They're screwing with us, Lily. That gun isn't ours."

Before Lily could consider that possibility, Coy asked her, "Didn't you love Jackson? How could you have had anything to do with his death?"

Before she could respond, Louie jumped to his feet and asked his mother the question that had been consuming both him and his brother, "Did you kill Dad, him and his friends?"

Both brothers fixed their mother with glares, awaiting an answer.

Annie raised a hand as if she were going to stand, lean across the table and slap her younger son — until John leaned forward, the Tommy gun pointed in Annie's direction.

"Unh-uh," he said. "No physical violence."

Annie sat back in her seat, her eyes cold and dark.

She said to John, "These three told us they wanted money. You for sale, too?"

John shrugged. No audio recorder would pick up that.

Annie turned her attention to the younger people. "How much do you want?"

Coy said, "I think that depends on how much you tell us. No answers, all the money."

Guy and Louie nodded, the older brother saying, "Yeah. That sounds fair."

Lily started to speak, but Annie held up a hand.

"Not a damn word out of you, Lily. That gun is *not* ours."

Lily leaned toward John. "It sure looks like it."

Annie ground her teeth. "Do I have to smack you again?"

"You try it and I'll knock your teeth out," Coy told her.

Annie turned to her sons. "Are you going to let her threaten me?"

Guy reminded her. "You haven't told us about Dad yet."

Both sisters sat mute. For a moment, they rested their shoulders against one another, a silent show of solidarity. They might have sat that way for some time if Coy hadn't started to laugh, and continued, slapping her hand on the table.

Guy and Louie looked at Coy as if maybe she was losing it.

In the end, it was Lily who felt compelled to speak.

"Are you all right, Coy?"

Annie rolled her eyes and leaned away from her sister.

Coy let her laughter peter out. "Me? I'm fine. Your sister just cracked me up, that's all. She reminded me of my own big sister. Doreen used to smack me around, too, when Mom and Dad were out of the house. Then, when it suited her, she acted like she was my best friend."

Annie sensed what Coy was doing. "Don't listen to her, Lily. She's trying to come between us."

John watched the by-play, waiting for an opportunity to buttress Coy's line of attack.

Coy gave one more laugh, short and sharp. "Yeah, Lily. Listen to Doreen there, like she's going to stick with you through thick and thin. Think about it, Lily. The cops have your confession."

John's moment had come. "We've also got you as an accomplice to Randy Bear Heart for everything he did. You took a loan against your business in Austin and bailed Randy out when his business was going under. The paper trail is there for anyone to see. You're an accomplice after the fact to all of Randy's crimes."

Annie's contempt for her sister's carelessness shone through once again.

"*There*," Coy said, pointing to Annie. "Did you see that look? That's exactly what Doreen would have done to me."

Lily was looking at Annie now, and unable to stop herself the older sister said, "You are so stupid."

That was when Lily broke. She pushed her chair away from Annie and pointed her finger at her. "She killed Vern and those other two. She paid Randy to do it, and he got some hooker to put something into that one boy's drink. She told me so."

Annie might have attacked Lily right then if John hadn't spoke up.

"We've got her anyway," he lied. "The money Harvey Kingsbury gave her was marked; the Canadian authorities were investigating him."

Sneering, Annie said, "Bullshit! I took Harvey's money and put it in the main office of my bank; I got money out of five other branches to pay Randy!"

Everyone sat there quietly. It took Annie a moment to realize she had just confessed to murder. She looked at her sons and Coy. "I'll give you a million dollars each to go away and forget all this."

"Yeah, you're good at sending people away," Louie said.

"What about him?" Guy asked, nodding in John's direction.

"Him?" Annie laughed. "He has no right to be here. He can't just walk into someone's home. Nothing he says will matter in court."

John shook his head.

"I do have a right to be here. I have an arrest warrant for Ms.

Lily White, aka Lily White Bird."

John put the Tommy gun on the table, stuck a hand in a pocket to get the warrant.

The automatic weapon lay halfway between the two sisters.

There for either of them to reach out and —

Colin McTee ran into the room and sized up the situation at a glance.

"Do *not* touch that damn thing!" the lawyer yelled.

John looked at the lawyer and thought, *Shit.*

Having Lily or Annie grab the Tommy gun would have been

—

"No!" McTee bellowed, even more alarmed now.

John turned and saw Annie pulling a handgun from under her shirt.

He'd taken his eye off the ball. No way was he going to get to the gun Bramley had given him. Not in time. He was sure Marlene Flower Moon must be laughing at him somewhere.

The Forger brothers, though, still trying to cope with their family tragedy, only had eyes for Mom. They jumped up and threw two solid hip checks into the dining room table. It slammed into Annie just as the gun cleared her waistband. A shot rang out and Annie went down.

The Tommy gun clattered to the floor but didn't discharge. It was unloaded.

Lily fell to her knees beside her sister and tried to stop the bleeding.

Guy went to see how he could help.

But Louie just turned to John and said, "Looks like we saved the day."

John asked him, "Yeah, you did, but who invited you to the party?"

CHAPTER 44

Banff, Alberta — July 19-26, the present

A search of the house on Muskrat Street disclosed that Annie Forger wasn't nearly as circumspect in her dealings with Randy Bear Heart as she would have people believe. She and Randy had liked to dine at restaurants in Las Vegas and other places where the patrons might avail themselves of having a photograph taken to preserve the memory of a happy occasion. Invariably, the two lovebirds sat side by side, smiling, with Randy's arm around Annie's shoulders.

As an accomplice after the fact to Randy's crimes, Annie was as cooked as any meal she'd ever eaten with the killer who'd fancied himself as an upgrade on Clyde Barrow.

Lily was ready to repent and repeated her confession to the RCMP and the FBI, but she had refused to say anything if John Tall Wolf was in the room. John had agreed to step out. He wasn't concerned about claiming credit. His career at the BIA didn't include the notion of rising in the organization.

He was interested, though, in reading the transcript of Lily's statement. She had elaborated on her original mea culpa. When Lily had called Jackson that night, she had only wanted him to take her out of her home and bring her somewhere safe. Randy had beaten her. It had been the first time he'd laid a hand on her. She thought it had shocked him as much as it had hurt her. He had run out of their house.

Jackson had arrived, wanted to bash his father when he'd seen what Randy had done to his mother, but Lily had told him that for the moment she just wanted to get away and persuaded him to help her pack some clothes. Randy had returned unexpectedly — just as they closed Lily's suitcase.

Father and son got into a fight. It raged throughout the house. Jackson was getting the better of it when Randy managed to grab an ax used to shave logs for the fireplace. He cleaved his son's skull with the blade.

John sighed. The image was horrible to imagine. Worse than getting clipped by a boat's propeller as he had first thought. Maybe as bad as leaving an infant for Coyote.

Randy had bought Lily's silence, initially, by threatening to testify against her for killing Daniel Red Hawk. It had helped Lily to rationalize her complicity in Jackson's death when Randy broke down in tears and grieved over his son's death. He said he'd loved the boy, had wanted him to become a famous musician. He told Lily that the two of them had to heal each other. She had believed that, because she wanted to. Randy had told her they had to be good to one another to get the job done.

He never went so far, though, as to tell her she would be his only woman.

The Bow River had claimed the sisters' Thompson submachine gun. It was never recovered. Superintendent Kent and other Mounties worried that some local person had claimed the weapon from the shallow waters of the river, and it would be the engine of future tragedies.

Neither Lily nor Annie would confess to causing Randy Bear Heart's death.

Every interrogator who worked on them got the impression both women still loved the man, and neither was ready to admit she'd been the agent of his death. There was still enough evidence to convict them on numerous other felonies.

Colin McTee, working with Canadian officials who would not deliver any prisoner they held to the United States to face capital punishment, negotiated a deal to have Lily tried by a tribal court at Mercy Ridge solely for causing the death of Officer Daniel Red Hawk and Annie to be tried as an ex post facto accomplice on the same charge. If found guilty, Canada would accept sentencing the sisters to life without parole.

The U.S. government would hold other murder charges in abeyance but not dismiss them, pending judgment and sentencing by the tribal court. Washington could live with a sentence of life without parole, too, but the government was taking no chances that Lily and Annie would game the system and go free.

Special Agent John Tall Wolf thought it a fair deal.

Marlene Flower Moon would have to become president and pardon Lily and Annie, before they'd ever get out of prison. Knowing Marlene, they'd have to wait until the final day of her second term in office to get the pardon. By that time, even Annie would be too old to commit further mayhem.

Canadian and U.S. authorities seized all the assets belonging to the two sisters, leaving Guy and Louie momentarily penniless. But their late father's former hockey team in Vancouver came through for the boys, buying the townhouse where they lived and allowing them to reside there until they graduated from college at which point they would be invited to tryouts with the team. If they were unable to qualify to be on the ice, other positions in the organization would be found for them.

There was never a determination made as to where the money found in Jackson White's safe deposit box had come from, and the money was returned to Coy Wilson. She gave it all to a home for abused children, not wanting any possible connection to Lily or Annie's karma to come back at her.

She kept Jackson's guitar and was busy writing one song after another. The music grapevine picked up stories she was producing great material. Country and pop music artists flooded her phone machine with requests to have first crack at Coy's new songs, but she was determined to record them herself.

Joseph Flynn

CHAPTER 45

Santa Fe, New Mexico — August 15, the present

As he always did between assignments, John Tall Wolf returned home. He spent a week in the wilderness with his mother and father learning to see things he'd never noticed before and sleeping under the stars. He shared what had happened with his parents. They were happy that he had come through the investigation unharmed, and no one else had suffered anything worse than being shot in the foot.

"Ms. Forger is going to have a lifetime limp," John said.

"And doubtless more atonement to face beyond this life," Serafina added.

Haden Wolf told his son, "Next time don't try to do everything yourself."

Dad was right, John thought. He should have had Rebecca Bramley with him at the house on Muskrat Street. She could have kept Colin McTee from rushing in and throwing him off his game.

The first night John was back at his house, Marlene Flower Moon pulled into the driveway in a Lexus. He stepped out the front door with his duty weapon in hand. He'd retrieved it from Darton Blake after filling the Austin detective in on what he'd missed.

The Texas cop had approved of the way things had been handled.

Not seeing any need for capital punishment.

"We've got way too many people getting killed in this country as it is; the good guys don't need to run up the score. Thanks for rounding out the story for me. You just inched up my opinion of federal lawmen."

John smiled. "Part of my mission, make friends everywhere I go."

Except, of course, with the woman for whom he worked.

Marlene saw the gun in John's hand and stopped ten feet away from him.

She waited to see if he put the Beretta in his waistband. He didn't.

"If not professional deference," she said, "you might show me a little common courtesy. Invite me in for a drink even."

John told her, "I don't bother you at home. Do you have another assignment for me?"

"I will, if I decide to keep you on."

"You'll give me a glowing reference if you don't?"

Marlene smiled and the moonlight gleamed on her incisors.

"I'd tell anyone just what they'd be dealing with, if they hired you."

John said, "I heard SAC Melvin was gracious enough to tell the media the case could not have been brought to a successful conclusion without the help of the BIA. Darton Blake even left a message on my phone machine that there was a photo of you, Melvin and Superintendent Kent on the front page of his morning newspaper. International cooperation and all that good stuff. You must be in clover in Washington and, with their sacred relics returned, at Mercy Ridge, too."

Marlene nodded. "My star is rising. You should keep that in mind."

"I certainly will," John said.

"I could take you places you've never been."

John wondered if she'd taken SAC Melvin a place or two. Overcome his better judgment and gotten him to have a drink or two with her and ... got him to share credit.

"Show me the kingdoms of the world?" John asked.

"Are you going to invite me in or not?" Marlene said.

As if in response to her question, Rebecca Bramley stepped into the open doorway to John's house. She wore hiking shorts and a man's shirt tied off just below her breast bone. She stepped outside and linked an arm with John's, the one that didn't end in his gun hand.

John made the introductions.

"Rebecca usually takes her summer holiday at home, but this year she thought she'd see a bit of the USA, outside of Florida. We thought we'd do a little touring and have a frank exchange of views on law enforcement."

Marlene did an about face any soldier — or Mountie — would have been proud of. She backed the Lexus out of the driveway and was gone in the blink of an eye. There was no screech of tires, roar of an engine or lingering exhaust fumes. She was simply gone in a blur.

For just a moment, John wondered if she'd gotten the better of him. Annie had been smarter than Lily about hiding her monetary connection to Randy Bear Heart. Marlene would have been much smarter than Annie about concealing any money she'd received from one or both sisters. If Marlene had decided her cash in hand was safe but Lily and Annie might cause her trouble down the road, having John put them in prison for life would suit her purposes beautifully.

After all, he'd first learned of Annie Forger's relationship with Randy Bear Heart by reading Randy's file … and who would have put that information there if not Marlene?

Rebecca said, "Woman sure knows how to make an exit, you have to give her that. You want to go back inside?"

John held up an index finger, asking her to wait.

For just a second before —

Concealed by the darkness, a coyote howled.

John couldn't tell whether the sound was plaintive or triumphant.

He was sure, though, his battles with Coyote were far from over.

ABOUT THE AUTHOR

Joseph Flynn has been published both traditionally — Signet Books, Bantam Books and Variance Publishing — and through his own imprint, Stray Dog Press, Inc. Both major media reviews and reader reviews have praised his work. Booklist said, "Flynn is an excellent storyteller." The *Chicago Tribune* said, "Flynn [is] a master of high-octane plotting." The most repeated reader comment is: "Write faster, we want more."

The Jim McGill Series
The President's Henchman, A Jim McGill Novel, #1
The Hangman's Companion, A Jim McGill Novel, #2
The K Street Killer, A Jim McGill Novel, #3
Part 1: The Last Ballot Cast, A Jim McGill Novel, #4
Part 2: The Last Ballot Cast, A Jim McGill Novel, #4
The Devil on the Doorstep, A Jim McGill Novel, #5
The Good Guy with a Gun, A Jim McGill Novel, #7
Short Cases 1-3, Three Jim McGill Short Stories

The Ron Ketchum Mystery Series
Nailed, A Ron Ketchum Mystery, #1
Defiled, A Ron Ketchum Mystery, 2

The John Tall Wolf Series
Tall Man in Ray-Bans, A John Tall Wolf Novel, #1
War Party, A John Tall Wolf Novel, #2

Other novels [continued on next page]

Round Robin, A Love Story of Epic Proportions
One False Step
Blood Street Punx
Still Coming
Still Coming Expanded Edition
Farewell Performance
Hot Type
Gasoline, Texas
The Next President
Digger
The Concrete Inquisition

If you would like to contact Joe, or read free excerpts of his books, please visit *www.josephflynn.com.*

CPSIA information can be obtained
at www.ICGtesting.com
Printed in the USA
BVHW030951171122
652109BV00009B/700